What You Don't Know Will Hurt You

Sara Coast

Printed in the United States of America
Book Broker Publishers of Florida
Port Charlotte, FL 33980
ISBN: 978-1-945690-14-3

What You Don't Know Will Hurt You

Sara Coast

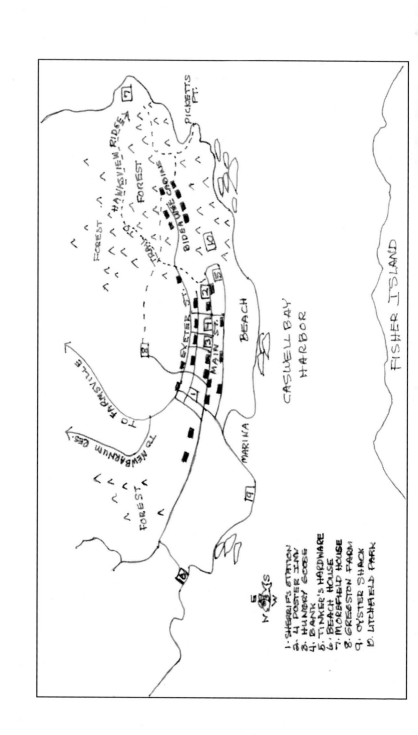

Prologue

The sun rose above the winter clouds, burning off the last of the morning fog. Melting icicles sparkled in the dawn's first rosy rays and disappeared into the wet snow. Seagulls wheeled and dived relentlessly searching for their morning meal in the icy waters.

Jake Mason stood on his front porch looking past the beach and the gulls, his eyes drawn toward Fisher Island. Through the last of the fog still blanketing most of the uninhabited island, he watched a light at the far south end flash, stop, flash again. On and off, on and off, rhythmically pulsating red, blue, and red. He wished he had his binoculars, thought about going back into the beach house to get them, but couldn't take his eyes off the lights. Fixated, he cupped his hands over his eyes and tried to focus. The flashing had stopped.

"Now what?" he muttered under his breath. He ran through the possibilities in his head. A fishing boat? No, that's what he thought last night when he saw the lights for the first time. Besides, the colors and pattern didn't add up to any kind of marine signal he was aware of. As his eyes squinted into horizontal slits scanning the length of the island, he could feel his neck muscles tighten, his heartbeat quicken. Just conditioned reflex, he thought. How important could they be, anyway? Nothing much ever happens around here. Why did seeing these lights cause him to feel so uneasy?

He adjusted his grey wool scarf tighter around his neck, pulled his coat collar up as high as it would go, and shoved his hands deep into his pockets. The chill in the cold winter wind forced him to move quickly down the last few steps of the beach house.

The sky brightened as the sun crested Hawksview Ridge. Sheriff Jake Mason climbed into his cruiser and headed to town.

One

Caswell Bay is a quiet place during the winter. While larger Maine cities bustle with activity, the Bay Township doesn't change much in the winter months. Most of the residents have lived there all their lives. The festive Christmas decorations bring out tourists from neighboring Bath and Brunswick and there's some ice fishing for the hardy.

But for Caswell Bay, late spring and summer promise more than just a rebirth of nature. Caswell Bay blossoms with an influx of tourists lusting for relaxation and quaintness, a touch of the past when things weren't as hectic. It seems as if the whole town comes alive as well. The town's hotel, motel, and guest houses are usually booked a year in advance for the annual Summerfair, held every July. Shopkeepers do very well.

In the center of Caswell Bay sits the 4-Poster Inn, a two-story colonial blue shingled Victorian house.

1

Like most Maine residents, the 4-Poster has withstood the elements and still stands weathered but proud, at 11 Main Street across from the harbor.

The front door opens into a large vestibule. The parlor to the right is a journey back in time with its heavily upholstered chairs, overstuffed couch, and love seat. A highly polished oak player piano sits waiting in the far corner. On the left is the dining room with its floor-to-ceiling glass doors opening out into a colorful flower garden. The wood staircase at the far end of the entry leads to the second-floor apartments.

In front of the Inn, purple hollyhocks and red geraniums will brighten up the white picket fenced in yard as soon as warm weather arrives. It's a cozy place indeed. The porch swing creaks happily when the owner, Marge Forstrum's two young nieces, nine and twelve, come for a visit; three weeks every summer, just like clockwork.

Across the street at the south end of the beach, stands 100-year-old Tinker's Hardware. A red brick walkway winds its way behind the store, ending at a set of wooden stairs. Below is a wide stretch of beach that wraps around the downtown area, ending near heavily wooded Pickett's Point about a mile farther south. In the summer months, it's nearly always filled with colorful umbrellas and deck chairs rented out by Tinker's hardware. Old man Tinker makes half his year's income from June to September. Small boats bob in the town's marina, north of the beach, where once was an amusement park that extended out into the water on a wood pier.

The beach is lined with huge glacial boulders and small smooth rocks in the waters below. Straight as an arrow, across the harbor from the marina about a half a mile out, lay one of the largest remnants of the Ice Age, Fisher Island. It was named for a Caswell banker's son who perished at Anzio in WWII. The mile-long rocky island rises ominously out of the bay. Its high craggy cliffs are usually filled with nesting birds.

At the far south end of the island stands Bay Harbor lighthouse, whose beacon warns boats and swimmers away from its treacherous shore.

Two

Clyde Dillon, Jake's chief deputy, slogged up the last few snow-covered stairs and entered the Caswell Bay Sheriff's Department. "Man, it's cold today," he muttered. "Is this winter ever gonna end?"

"Hey, Tina," he said sticking his head through a half-open door into the dispatcher's office. "Coffee on yet?"

"You bet, Clyde, on and ready. Where you been?"

"Had to shovel out again this morning. The neighbor's kids couldn't get to the bus."

Coffee in hand, Clyde looked around the room. He could already feel the warmth of the department thawing him out. Sergeant Sam Owens was going over the daily work schedule with Deputy Ben Clemens. One of the other deputies, Chuck Jackson, was in Barnstable checking on a car that went missing from someone's driveway yesterday. But no Jake.

He stuck his head back in the door again. "Tina, seen the Chief yet?"

"Nope. Didn't call in, so he must be on his way."

"Thanks," he said and settled down to catch up on yesterday's unfinished problems. He started sorting through the piles of papers on his desk. He sighed. The Cutter's boy's bike report. He was sure he had left it right on top. Now where was it?

Clyde has always lived in Caswell Bay. He and Jake hit it off right away when Jake first came to the Bay from California a little over five years ago. They've been best friends ever since. Clyde helped him through the illness and death of his father. Jake admired him a great deal. He was getting worried about Jake. He needed to get out more. Since his Dad died, his work was his life.

"Tina. Do you know what happened to Bobby's lost bike report? I can't find it."

"I put it in your wire basket. Look, right there on top," she said with a grin.

"Hey, Clyde," Sheriff Mason called out as he stamped his feet, showering snow everywhere. Everyone looked up from what they were doing.

"Clyde, What're you doing?" Jake asked as he watched Clyde rummage through his desk. "Lose your million-dollar lottery ticket?"

"C'mon Jake. It's early yet. Give me a break."

Sam, sitting at his desk near the water cooler just shook his head and laughed. He and Tina, who were used to the two men ribbing each other, sat back and enjoyed the free show.

"I was just trying to find a report on Bobby Cutter's missing bike," Clyde said. "Seems somebody swiped the bike the other night. Can't imagine anyone in town doing that. Seen anyone suspicious hanging around? And by the way, what makes you so cheery this morning?"

"I don't know," Jake said. "Maybe it's the thought all this snow and cold will be gone in a couple of months. But, about that bike, if you'd unchain yourself from that desk, you could answer that question yourself. You work too hard on stuff that can wait 'til tomorrow. Does Esther even know you when you come home?"

Clyde responded. "Look who's talking, Mr. Workaholic."

"That's calling the kettle black," Tina said.

Jake strode over to Tina's office. "Hey Tina, have you had any calls come in about those flashing lights out near Fisher Island? I saw them early this morning again, that's the second time now. Somebody else must've spotted them. They have a strange pattern, sort of a bright red, then changing to blue and back to red again."

Tina opened her mouth, a smile already in place.

Jake cut her off. "Before you say it, they're not leftover Christmas lights."

She laughed.

"They sure don't match any marine signal I'd ever seen either," Jake said. He turned to his second in command. "Clyde, maybe we should get the boat out and take a look."

"No, please, Jake. Don't get crazy on me. You've been watching too many sci-fi movies"

"Yeah, well, probably nothing to get excited about. I'm going to keep an eye out just the same," Jake said. "When we get a calm day, I'm going out there."

He checked his desk for messages, then stepped back into the open area of the office. "I'll be glad when this cold spell lifts. It is just too damn cold for March and too much snow. Tina, anything come in that needs my attention right away? If not, I'm going down to the Hungry Goose for breakfast."

"No, Chief."

"OK. Call me if you need me. I won't be long. Clyde, want anything?"

"Sure, bring me back a coupla doughnuts and Bobby's bike."

Jake decided to walk the two blocks despite the below-freezing weather. He needed the exercise. The sun had only been up a couple of hours. He turned right toward Main Street. Reaching the corner, he glanced to his left down the street, still pretty empty. A milk delivery truck sat in front of the 4-Poster. Across the street, he saw Herman Clark and his hound dog Millie out for their morning constitutional and waved. It reminded him of how quiet Caswell Bay is in the winter and early spring months.

He hadn't gone two car lengths, when he spotted a shiny red chrome Sportsmaster bike leaning against a parking meter. Well, what do you know, he thought. Must be Bobby's lucky day.

Jake checked out the bike for damage. All looked fine. He gripped Bobby's pride and joy under the cross bar and rolled it down the cleared sidewalk until it was at the foot of the steps of the department. He ran up the steps, opened the door a crack and called over to Clyde.

"Hey, I've got a present for you. Come here and take a look."

7

Clyde stared down at the bike at the foot of the steps and just shook his head.

"Unbelievable. Hope you solve your flashing light mystery just as fast," he said laughing as he watched Jake carry the bike up into the station.

Three

On his way down the street, Jake almost collided with Turner Ward, the rookie who'd just joined them. He liked Turner's enthusiasm and youthful dedication. He reminded Jake of when he first joined the force back in California.

"Oh, sorry, sheriff. I was running late and…" he said breathlessly.

"It's OK, slow down, be back soon," Jake said. "Go talk to Clyde. He has your assignment for today."

As Turner pushed open the front door, he almost fell over the bike leaning against the wall near the entry.

"What's up with the bike?" he called over to Clyde, who was headed back to his desk.

"It was lost, and the great detective, Jake Mason, found it down the street," he laughed. "Exciting, right?"

"The Chief tracked down a missing bike? Turner looked incredulous. "Come on, doesn't he have more important stuff to do?"

"Hey, don't bad talk the Chief," Tina snapped.

"Yeah, rookie," Sam chimed in. "What do you know, you just got here."

Turner's face turned red. "No, I didn't mean to…"

"Hey, get off the guy's back," Clyde said. "Seriously, Turner, the Chief is just on top of stuff. That's just the way he is." Pulling up a chair in front of Turner's work station, Clyde sat down.

"I mean, I wasn't insulting him, it's just that I see him as being way up there and a bike? I'd like to get to know him better, Clyde, and you've been here the longest. If you have a moment, could you tell me about the sheriff?"

"For one thing, he's quite a guy. Jake used to be a police lieutenant out in L.A. He came here a few months before his Dad died."

"Wasn't that a big change for the sheriff?" Turner asked. "I mean, the excitement of life in a California station sure wouldn't compare with life in the Bay.

"I'll say," Sam spoke up.

"Yeah, well, you're right about that," Clyde said. "Jake had been in the line of fire for a lot of years. Like one day, on his day off, he just happened to be in his neighborhood deli, down the street from a bank—"

Sam pulled his chair in. Tina put down the reports she was working on and joined them. The excitement in Clyde's voice had them fixated.

"Jake had just paid for the wine. He noticed a blue Mustang parked in the no parking zone in front of the bank. The motor was running and a young man was behind the wheel. He noticed the kid's especially bushy eyebrows and thought he looked like a cartoon character, you know the one, the guy with the big eyebrows and the cigar—"

"Oh, yeah," Sam said and they all laughed. Ben had stopped what he was doing and sat with his feet up on an adjoining desk.

"Well anyway just then, he saw the armored car coming down the street for its usual pickup," Clyde continued. "Something wasn't right. When the armored car stopped, the driver opened the door. By the time the door closed, the kid was on him holding a sawed off shotgun in his face. The kid took the driver's revolver and forced him up the bank steps and through the front door."

Turner let out an audible gasp. "Holy—!"

Clyde's audience didn't move.

"Well, then Jake sprung into action. He told the storekeeper to call 911, pulled out his service revolver and started toward the bank. Stooped low on the landing outside the windowed front door, he was able to see the robber had the bank's bags in one hand. With his other hand, the kid waved the shotgun around threatening everyone to stay down on the floor."

"Jake could hear the sirens in the distance. The robber was slowly backing toward the front door, when Jake glanced back over his shoulder. There was another man in the car, who was leaning out of the back window aiming a shotgun straight at Jake. Jake swiveled around and fired one shot at the man in the car, who returned fire."

"The shot passed by Jake, went through the bank

door and hit the first robber in the back of the neck dropping him to the floor. Jake fired again toward the car and was down the stairs and had the gunman on the ground by the time the patrol cars arrived on the scene."

"Wow!" Turner said.

"I don't know if I could have —" Ben started to say as the front door opened.

Jake looked over at the six of them still gathered around Clyde's desk.

"What's the big conference about?"

Turner jumped up like a jack in the box, almost knocking over his chair.

"Take it easy, rookie," Clyde said. "Turner here wanted to get to know you better and I was telling them of one of your California stories."

"Oh, not the bank robber story again." Jake just shook his head and went into his office.

Four

Jake spotted a robin perched on one of the green park benches placed along the sidewalks on each side of the street. He couldn't believe it was the first of June already. The winter had dragged on, keeping many townspeople housebound and edgy. Now spring has finally managed to open the door. Life has returned to Caswell Bay. Red and white geranium-filled hanging flower baskets swing from the wrought-iron lamp posts. The leaves of the maples lining Main Street now reach out their newly unfolded leaves, promising shade for the summer tourists.

This morning, the sun rose over the inlet, its warmth burning off the morning fog in the cove between the beach and Fisher Island. Beyond the houses, Jake could barely see the yellow buoy light at the south end of the island, bobbing in the water. Earlier that week, he'd again taken the skiff and covered the area between the beach and Fisher Island. He'd docked the boat near the lighthouse on the south end of the island where he'd seen the lights. He found nothing unusual. The lights seemed to have stopped. At least no one had reported seeing them.

Jake, standing in front of Tinker's Hardware, looked out toward the fog-bound island again. There was something ominous about it. Even the sea lions no longer sat out on the bare rocks anymore and Jake never saw seagulls wheeling over the island or perched on the scraggly bushes. It used to be a favorite nesting site.

The west side of the island was still closed off due to the overabundance of red algae and seaweed growing in the water. The townspeople were warned not to go out to the island until the mayor and the council decided what to do about the problem. Signs were posted to keep out swimmers and small boats were forbidden access. Few local people ever went there anyway; it wasn't at the top of their agenda.

He turned and started into the hardware store catching a last glimpse of the island in the plate glass window as he entered, letting the screen door slam behind him. Jake felt a chill run through his body.

Five

As he stood outside smoking a cigarette, Major Anton Vorack stared up at the endless carpet of stars covering the clear night sky. Vorack was pleased to feel the warm spring air at last and breathed deeply, letting the saltiness of the ocean air fill his lungs. He rarely went outside. This was a treat for him. The mission was coming close to an end. He inhaled the last of the cigarette and crushed it with his foot on the hard glacial rock on which he stood.

Back inside, Vorack called to a guard to bring Dimitri Povash to his office. He poured himself a vodka and waited. A few moments later, a young man dressed in black entered and sat facing him in the Major's office, a small room on the first floor adjacent to one of the six labs on the premises. He stared unflinchingly into Dimitri's eyes, sensing his self-assurance and strength. The Major smiled like a hawk sizing up his prey. Dimitri wasn't tall, but very muscular. He'd do very well.

Dimitri's gaze never left the Major. He'd arrived that morning and already had determined he didn't like the confines of the cave like facility he'd be spending time in on this assignment. He'd heard a lot about this maniac. He didn't like the Major, but he didn't have a choice. He had to follow his orders. He'd watch his back. He'd get through this.

Vorack had only a hint of an accent. He made himself speak only English since his arrival in the United States ten years ago. He had good dialect coaches. He tried to insist the other workers speak only English. He wanted them to blend in. That was vitally important.

"Welcome, Dimitri. I trust Karl has shown you around our fine facility. We also trust you'll get to know your way around here shortly."

The Major pushed a photo across the table to Dimitri.

"Have you ever heard of a man named Jake Mason, now Sheriff Jake Mason of the Caswell Bay Sheriff's Department?"

Dimitri shook his head. "How does he fit in? Is he part of the mission?"

The Major just smiled "Later. Here's an envelope with information on an agent who will be joining you shortly. I need a background check by tomorrow morning. We'll talk again then. I have work to do now. Go."

"Yes sir," Dimitri replied.

As Dimitri climbed the stairs to the second floor records room, he wondered how he was going to get along with this sly, manipulative Major Vorack he'd been warned about.

He followed the empty corridor to the main

operations room and pressed a switch on the wall. The row of incandescent lights on the ceiling flickered, went out, and then filled the room with light.

He went over to the computer, turned it on and typed in a message to Major Krazinsky back in Kazakhstan. Kraz always knew everything about what was going on in the organization.

He pressed send and sat back in his chair and waited. He looked at the clock above the closed door. "Hmm, maybe it's too early." He'd just closed his eyes when he heard the printer come to life.

Pulling the sheet out of the tray, he thought, that's my boy, Kraz. He looked down and started to read the copy.

Downstairs, the Major looked at his calendar. It was June 22nd already. Major Vorack knew he only had eighteen days until Summerfair. There was a lot to do before then. He was getting anxious, but he'd never allow anyone to see it. He went into a room adjacent to his office.

Only two overhead lights remained on, one flickering, dimming and then going out, giving the room an eerie glow. Everyone had retired for the night except security positioned outside the complex. Vorack sat staring at the computer monitor, lines of encryption cascaded down the screen. He finally pressed the close key and the screen went dark. Yes, he had done a good night's work. He'd talk to Dimitri first thing in the morning. Dimitri had better have the information on the agent. Vorack liked to test new agents on their ability to follow orders.

The sun would be up in an hour. He prepared to

head down the corridor toward the kitchen area to see if someone had eaten that last piece of apple pie. Then he'd be off to his quarters and try to sleep if only for a short time.

He glanced over at one of the security monitors still lit and saw the man he counted on the most, Yuri Petrenko. He'd been a brilliant choice for the task. At least something was going right.

Six

As Vorack tried to fall asleep he recalled his history with Petrenko.

He could still see the lab technicians formed in a circle around a wide metal table in the center of the dimly lit room hidden deep underground on Fisher Island. He could see Dr. Petrenko coldly staring at him from one end of the table. He was holding a shiny silver oblong cylinder in each hand. He knew the highly moral Petrenko hated him. But he didn't care. The contents of those cylinders were his destiny.

Petrenko had pushed his patience to the limit. At that moment, he had only a little more than three months until Summerfair began. Summerfair was just the distraction he needed for a successful mission. He told Petrenko his life would be over if the invention failed and he meant it.

Petrenko was weak, defensive, and bitchy. The

major recalled the scientist's reply when he told him to hurry. Vorack remembered Petrenko had had the gall to say "perhaps you could do better yourself, Major." If he hadn't needed him so much, he would have shot the scientist.

Fortunately for Petrenko, the invention did work, and work beautifully. The replay in his brain of the demonstration filled Vorack with so much excitement, his eyes opened wide. He could actually see it in front of him as if it were yesterday.

Petrenko pressed the red button on one of the cylinders releasing his metallic birdlike flying invention. It hovered over the lab table, suddenly disappearing from sight. A small glass tube appeared out of nowhere and fell into a beaker of water. The tube exploded upon entering the beaker and a red liquid was released into the water.

What an invention! He was ecstatic all over again, imagining how this small amount of released chemical had the capacity of poisoning an entire city water system. The chemical when added to water would replicate itself every five minutes until its potency would contaminate any reservoir it entered, in its entirety, within twenty hours.

Vorack sat straight up in bed overcome with excitement just thinking about it.

Yes, he thought, a quick and lethal annihilation, no loss of military lives, little cost compared to an all-out visible attack. He would make millions on this one.

Petrenko had also put together another version containing a surveillance camera able to send real time photos. It could even be released in a building and could mount itself on a wall, invisible and undetected, and record whatever is being said or seen.

Vorack fell back onto the bed, letting his head sink into the soft pillow. Who could possibly imagine such an invention in 1998? People would think it was an alien invasion, who knows. A self-satisfied smile formed on the Major's face. He drifted off thinking of the possibilities. After demonstrating the capabilities of the device to the right people, he could open it up to the highest bidder. Finally he'd be out of his damp, dreary dungeon and be living in luxury. Eighteen days until Summerfair didn't sound like a lot of time. He hoped all would be ready.

Seven

Marge Forstrum, owner of the 4-Poster Inn, busied herself arranging a bouquet of spring lilacs on the dining room table. Lilacs were always her favorite flower. She was humming quietly and didn't notice a young woman entering the room.

"Good morning, Marge," Grace said in a cheery voice.

"Good morning to you, Ms. Cooper." Marge looked up, surprised. "I didn't hear you come in. How was your night?"

"It was fine, thanks," Grace replied. "I saw a dog outside. Is he yours?"

"Oh, that's Maxie. He sometimes barks at Betsy, the neighbor's cat when she goes prowlin' at night. I hope he didn't keep you awake."

"No, I slept like a baby. Any chance I could get something to eat?"

It wasn't long before Marge returned with bacon

and eggs and homemade biscuits.

"I made the jam myself. I love to go blueberry pickin in the summa'."

Marge made them a pot of tea and sat down with Grace.

"Well, it says on the register you'll be with us awhile. I like to get to know my guests and let em know a little about me as well."

"Sure. What would you like to know?"

"Whatever you wish, my dear."

"Well, let's see. I've been working in a college library in Boston, but I'm originally from Holworth, Nebraska."

"Boston?" Marge replied. "How'd you get out east? Why Boston?"

"Well, that's a long story." Grace laughed. "Let's just say the job offer was good. Anyway, I took a journalism course and began writing freelance magazine pieces about unusual events around the country."

"My lands," Marge said. "Tell me, dear, what's so unusual about Caswell Bay?"

"Now I can't tell you everything, you'll have to read about it," Grace said, smiling broadly.

"Well, you are being mysterious," Marge said. "Good luck with your story. Be sure and spell my name correctly." Marge laughed and went into the kitchen with the empty dishes.

It occurred to Grace that Marge had told her nothing about herself. Grace called after her, but she was gone.

Grace went back up to her room and pulled her suitcase out from under the bed. She opened it and took out a brown leather briefcase. She spilled out the contents on top of her bedcover.

This certainly has proven to be invaluable, she thought as she found the map of the Caswell Bay area. She searched for the photos she'd taken earlier the day before and spread them out on the bed. She retrieved a magnifying glass and looked carefully at the terrain on Fisher Island.

She wanted to check around to hear what people were saying about flashing lights. She wanted to meet the sheriff. Let's see, she thought, what was his name? Oh yes, Jake Mason. He could help her. She knew that in a few days she'd feel more at ease in Caswell Bay. She opened a manila folder and reread the contents.

Grace returned the items to the briefcase, which she now stored on top of the polished oak wardrobe. Before she left the room, she went over to a white porcelain bowl filled with fresh water on the lace-covered dresser. She splashed a little of the cool water on her face and dried herself with a small towel.

Looking up at the mirror on the stand, she caught her image staring back. Don't forget who you are, a voice inside reminded her.

"How could I forget? I'm Grace, Grace Cooper," she answered, smiling at her likeness. She liked her name, Grace. It was her grandmother's name. It made her feel that her grandmother was watching over her, protecting her. She liked that.

She started down the stairs and almost ran into a man in a green uniform who was obviously in a hurry.

"Sorry, late for work," he threw at her on his way down the stairs. "Name's Turner, ma'am, Deputy

Turner Ward."

"Grace," she blurted out, caught up in the young man's hurry, "Grace Cooper."

"Talk to you later, ma'am. Nice meeting you," he called, the front screen door banging loudly behind him.

Well, I'll bet he knows Sheriff Jake Mason, Grace smiled, and closed the door behind her.

She walked down the maple-lined streets of Caswell Bay to the town library. When Grace arrived, she asked the librarian for the local newspaper files from 1990 up to the present. Seated in front of a microfiche, Grace moved quickly through the headlines.

The first article that caught her eye was dated May 22, 1991. It's headline: **Russian Oil Tanker Runs Aground**. It read:

> Sometime in the night the Russian oil tanker *Levongrad* ran aground near Fisher Island. The company refuses to let any locals help in its removal. In fact, they were very unfriendly toward any boat or anyone who approached the tanker. Their owner assured the local police that no oil had leaked out and that they would have it out of the waters within a week's time. Sheriff Reimer encouraged people to stay away and let the company handle the problem.

An article dated Sept. 19, 1991 also caught her eye. Its headline: **Red Tide Reaches Maine?** It read:

> Marine biologist Gill Post of the Coulter Institute was called to our fair city to check out the mysterious occurrence of red algae growth on the west side of Fisher Island. Fortunately, it

25

seemed to be staying there, preventing our local beaches from being polluted with the stuff and the smell that goes with it. Dr. Post stated he had two theories for the unusual arrival. He said an unexplained change of water temperature was noted as well as a chemical shift in the salinity. He researched Maine's geological history and said it was possible that a small fissure had opened in the sea bottom on the west side of the island allowing heat to escape into the water. He said more research was needed. Mayor Wilkes had declared the island off limits to locals and the curious as well until further notice.

The next article was dated Aug. 12, 1992. It's headline: **Violent Storm Hits Caswell Bay**.

Last night about 3 a.m., the predicted violent storm became a reality, creating widespread damage to the harbor here at Caswell Bay. Waking up to a calm, sunshiny day, citizens were shocked to see the local pier was damaged heavily, Lawson's bait shop under two feet of water and many boats that had been tied up at the dock, stacked like cordwood. Fortunately, no one was injured except Pete Small, who tripped over his cat while trying to find safe shelter. The rocky shoreline was left mostly safe. Clean up will take weeks. Unfortunately, the storm did not dissipate the heavy algae still clogging up the west side of Fisher Island. The winds hit hurricane force, gusting to 85 miles an hour. People talked about what sounded like an explosion, the ground shuddered as the waves grew three to five feet along the shoreline. This wasn't the first time they heard the loud noises, several residents said. It was usually in conjunction with a storm or in the early morning hours. It was always accompanied by heavy wave action. No one could ever pinpoint the source of the noise.

In the next two days, wherever Grace went, she casually asked about 1992. Old Mrs. Shaw at the five and dime, concurred that 1992 was quite a year for Caswell Bay. Beside the many strange events, locals were all atwitter with stories of alien sightings and strange lights at night. It wasn't until the next summer, she said, that people settled down to their usual routines.

"What with them tourists comin' back, and Summafair and all, that algae's awful out there I hear," she said, bending close to a rare audience. "Why don't they make it look tourist friendly. I don't know why they don't get rid of that muck. Maybe we need a new mayor."

Grace managed to ease toward the door of the shop.

"Oh well," Mrs. Shaw concluded, "the tourists still come."

Grace thanked her and thought, interesting. A whole lot of complaints, but no action. That's really curious. Well, better get to work.

Eight

Jake's eyes did a quick scan of the diner, looking for Clyde and Sam. He noticed a young man in a hoodie drinking coffee in a back booth. Their eyes met for a moment; the man averted his gaze. He looked out of place for some reason. Jake was about to approach him, but then he caught Clyde waving at him.

The booths, reminiscent of a lot of 50's diners, were covered in red plastic. Juke box selectors hung on the wall side of the tables next to the catsup bottles. Dolores Torres was standing next to the booth taking Clyde's order. Jake slid in next to Sam.

"So, what's it today, Jake?" she chirped.

"I'll just have the usual."

"Thought you might. One day you'll surprise me, sheriff."

After she left, Clyde leaned over close to Sam. "I can see why you like her, Sam. When you gonna ask her out? Now that's the question."

Clyde loved to tease Sam. He'd known Sam since they were in high school.

Sam blushed. He was a really nice guy, but shy when it came to women.

"Ease up on this boy, Clyde."

Clyde laughed and said, "Sorry, Sam, I remember the teasing I got when I was trying to get Esther to go out with me."

"You all save room for something sweet?" Dolores asked when they were done. "None for you, Clyde, you doughnut junkie," she teased.

She looked over at Sam. "How about you, deputy?"

Sam turned red as a beet and just shook his head.

Jake tried not to laugh.

"Guess not, just the bill."

Sam got up. "I'm never eating with the two of you jokesters again. I've got to get back to the department. Chuck and I have to get over to Farmsville. See ya later."

"Don't get lost." Jake called after him.

Sam just waved and just shook his head.

Clyde wiped the last of the doughnut crumbs from his mustache. "Say Jake, did I tell you that I got a call yesterday about someone seeing flashing lights near the lighthouse? Meant to mention it. A couple of months ago you seemed nuts to find out about the lights you saw."

"Clyde, are you pulling my leg?"

"No," said Clyde, "It's true. Some guy named Bob Fulmer noticed the lights when he was birdwatching up on Hawksview Ridge, just before sunset. I thought of you right away. Sorry. Don't

29

know why I forgot to tell you."

"It's OK, Clyde." Jake looked off through the plate-glass window of the diner. "What do you know, the lights have started up again. The big question is why did they start to begin with. Did you get his number?"

"It's on my desk," answered Clyde. Good luck finding it, he thought. "You ever been up on the Ridge? You get a spectacular view of Fisher Island from there."

"No, not yet. But, I heard some stories about the old house up there. Sounded creepy. Are they true?"

"What'd you hear?"

"I was in the hardware store one day and noticed a picture above the cash register," Jake said. "Old man Tinker said it was Randolph Morefield. The Morefields ran everything in town at one time."

"That's right," Clyde said. "My folks used to talk about them like they were kings and queens up there."

"Tinker said, even before he was born, they lived in a big house up on Hawksview Ridge. He said the last one, I think he said her name was Alice, just closed up the place one day about twenty years ago. She didn't pack up anything and was never seen again. Weird story. You've lived here a long time. Is it true?"

"Yeah, that's about what we all grew up hearin'," Clyde said. "You'd believe it, too, if you saw the place inside. I went back up there about six years ago. A fisherman called into the station, saying he was about a half mile out heading towards the marina late one night and thought he'd saw a light in one of the windows."

"Did you find anything suspicious?"

"No, but Jake, you really ought to go up there and see for yourself. It's creepy alright. It doesn't smell so hot either. Everything's covered with dust and cobwebs—the dining room table with the lace cover still on it, the plates in the cupboards, the dishes still in the sink in the kitchen. The closets are still full of clothing, just hanging there in shreds. We checked everything, but couldn't get into the basement area. It was locked. We'd seen enough. It didn't matter."

"Did anyone find out why she left?"

"Nope."

"C'mon, let's get the check and get back. I want to talk to this guy."

Jake paid the bill and they started to leave.

"I think I'll take a hike up to the Ridge myself and look around. Maybe, I'll get lucky and catch some light activity myself. I'll check around the house too, while I'm up there."

"Listen, Jake. It is so beautiful up there. Even if nothing turns up, you won't regret it. At the highest point on Hawksview Ridge you can see far out to sea. There are maples, oaks, fir trees. I love the smell of the firs. Reminds me of Christmas. Now that summer's here, there'll be wildflowers blooming along the path leading down to the clearing below. I don't know why I haven't been back since."

"Clyde, you sound like a poet," joked Jake.

"Well, anyway, I took the kids camping there when they were little. You'll see it when you come out of the forest. We had fun picking wild blueberries. The bushes are everywhere. When the weather's just right, it's a great place to lie in the tall grass and watch the clouds roll by."

"You sold me Clyde. Come on. I want to make that call to Fulmer."

"Oh, and Jake, Esther wants you to come for dinner on Sunday. She asked me if you'd stop at the video store and pick up a movie for after dinner. She said pick something romantic for a change and she didn't mean Bonnie and Clyde."

Jake laughed. "Sounds great, I like her sense of humor. Count me in."

Nine

Back at the department, Jake leaned back in his office chair and waited as Larry Fulmer's phone rang and rang.

"Fulmer's Grain and Feed," someone finally answered. "Larry speaking. What can I do for you?"

"Mr. Fulmer, this is Sheriff Mason over in Caswell Bay. I received a report that you witnessed a series of flashing lights coming from Fisher Island. Is that correct? And, can you tell me more about what you saw?"

"Yes, I was on my way down from Hawksview Ridge. Let me see, hmm yeah, it was late Sunday. I'd been up on the Ridge bird watching. I was watching a sparrow hawk fly toward the west and picked up a flash of light. It looked as if it was coming from Fisher Island. It was odd—red and then blue and then red again. By the time I got a better view, it had stopped. I thought maybe somebody was in trouble. I called the nearest station and talked with one of your deputies."

"You're talking about last Sunday, right?

Sunday, June 19th. Is that correct?"

"Yes, I'm off on the weekend."

"Anything else you can tell me? Did you see anyone while you were in the area?"

"No... well, yes. I saw a young man on my way down back to town. He was dressed in black and wore a grey hoodie. Oh, yes, He wore a backpack. I don't think he saw me. It was a distance away. He looked as if he was headed up to the Ridge. Don't know why anyone would go up that time of day. Was I any help, Sheriff?"

Well, Jake thought. He remembered the man he'd seen earlier at the diner and made a note of that. "Thanks so much for you time, Mr. Fulmer. We'll be in touch if we have any more questions."

After he hung up, Jake's wheels began to turn. Time for another excursion to the island, he thought. Jake popped his head into Tina's office. "Clyde, Sam, and I are going to take the patrol boat out to the island for a looksee. We should be back before dark. Oh, by the way, where were you at lunch? I thought you were going to join us."

"Oh, I was there, but in the kitchen talking to Floyd, you know, the new cook," Tina said. "He's my friend, Martha Jones' nephew. Anyway, listen, Chief, I saw the cutest guy at the takeout counter. Wow, he had such big beautiful brown eyes. He looked like fisherman, you know, plaid shirt, denim jeans and grey jacket that had a hood."

"You said a grey hooded jacket?" Jake queried.

"Yeah, but, he didn't have the hood up. He was wearing a New York Mets cap. I noticed that even though he had a deep tan and looked rugged, he had manicured finger nails. Lois and her manicures make me more aware of people's nails. Crazy. When he picked up his hamburger, he argued with the clerk about his change. He had a slight accent. I couldn't quite place it. Sort of European, I think. After he left I asked Meg if she knew who he was. She thought he was probably just a tourist who was renting one of the Bide a Wee Cabins near Overlook Beach. The fishermen like to hang out there." Tina laughed. "With any luck, I might run into him again. I like mysterious guys."

"Yeah. You probably will. I noticed the same man when I was there and he was seated in the back, wearing the hood then. Actually, the Fulmer man I just talked to saw someone bearing his description going up toward Hawksview Ridge recently. He must get around. Good luck."

Jake shook his head. For a smart woman, Tina sometimes sure took the long way to get to a point. He motioned to Clyde.

"Hey Clyde, head on down to the marina and get the patrol boat ready. You and I are going out to Fisher Island."

"Again?"

"Yes, again."

"Tina, what's the weather report for today?"

"Looks good now, Chief. A storm is due to hit late this evening though. You'll be back well before then."

"OK. Sam, I want you to come too. We need an extra pair of eyes. We should be back by five. You can reach me on the boat radio."

"Take care now," Tina called after them.

As Jake approached the dock, Clyde already had the motor running.

"Head for the south end of the island first, then we'll do a full circle around. Maybe this time, we'll find something."

By the time they reached the south end of the island, the wind started to pick up. Small whitecaps rode the crests of each building wave. The boat bobbed up and down. The jagged shore didn't look friendly, so they stayed at sea at a safe distance and used binoculars to scan the rocky outcropping. Again, nothing of note on the south end.

As the wind began to increase, they circled around on the west side of the island, staying out of range of the drifting algae. The storm appeared to be moving faster toward them. As they were rounding the north end to head back to the marina, Jake spotted a small skiff with one occupant headed toward the island.

"Clyde, I think we'd better intercept it. We need to tell the person the island's off limits. Must be one of the new tourists."

Clyde headed the patrol boat toward the skiff at full speed. Jake turned on the siren and spotlight.

Grace, concentrating on her path to the island, looked up just in time to see a boat in the distance headed on a collision course with hers. Then she thought she heard a siren and saw the searchlight aimed in her direction.

"Oh, damn," she said. "It's the sheriff's patrol boat. What bad luck."

As the lawmen pulled alongside the skiff, Jake yelled down to Grace through a megaphone.

"Are you headed to the island?"

"Yes," Grace yelled back.

"Don't you know the island is off limits? It looks

as if the storm's coming in early. Go back to the marina. We'll follow you and be sure you get there safely."

"Thanks," she yelled back.

Back at the dock, Jake told Clyde and Sam to finish tying down the boat. He wanted to talk with the woman. Clyde and Sam just smiled at each other. Even wet from the spray, she was easy to look at.

Jake saw the woman coming toward him. She was tall and slim, in her thirties, he guessed, wearing a light blue nylon jacket and white shorts. Jake didn't miss her shapely tanned legs. When he reached out his hand and introduced himself, he also took in her clear green eyes. She was stunning.

"Hello, I'm Sheriff Jake Mason. Listen, sorry to cut you off like that. It was for your own protection. You should have received a booklet at the marina about Fisher Island. What were you doing out there anyway, if you don't mind my asking."

Grace seemed flustered. Jake Mason. Well, it wasn't the way she would have planned their first meeting.

"Sheriff, so sorry to cause trouble," she said, freeing her long blonde ponytail from her scarf, "It was my first trip out to the island. I wanted to go there to do some research. My name is Grace Cooper. I'm a magazine writer."

"Well, Ms. Cooper. I'm happy you're all right. I have to ask, though, what would be interesting enough in our small town to pique your interest?"

"Grace, please. I was just going out to see if I

could get any evidence of the flashing lights phenomenon."

"Really? Where did you hear about that?"

Grace noted how the sheriff reacted when she mentioned the lights. Hmmm. "From a newspaper article about a month ago."

"OK, well, at least you're back here safe and sound."

"Sheriff, if you don't mind, I'd like to interview you. I'd like to ask you some questions about the lights and anything unusual you've observed in the area. I know this isn't the right time to approach you, but here we are."

Boy, he thought. She's brassy as well as beautiful.

"Tell you what, Ms. Cooper. Why don't you come down to the department when you get changed? I'll be happy to talk with you. The Sheriff's Department is on Beldon Street, just off of Main."

"Thanks, Sheriff. I'll do that," Grace said, then turned and hurried on up the ramp.

"I can't believe it. You're hitting on her, Sheriff Mason," Clyde snickered. "What's your next move when she gets to the station?"

"What do you mean? We'll talk. Maybe she'll have some insight into the weird lights, maybe something we've missed."

"Right," said Clyde, laughing all the way to the cruiser.

When they arrived back at the department, Tina looked at them.

"Were you able to find anything new?"

Jake was still in the doorway. "Nope," he replied.

"Jake, why's Clyde laughing. Something funny happen?"

"Normally, I'd tell you to ask Clyde, but just let it go for now. I'm expecting a Grace Cooper to arrive shortly. Send her to my office. Thanks."

"Will do," answered Tina, her curiosity raised to the max. She'd get it out of Clyde before the day was over. But an hour later, she didn't have to. Grace showed up in the department and Tina directed her toward Jake's office. She saw Jake offer her a seat and smiled, making eye contact with him for a moment before he closed the door. So that's it, she said to herself.

"Thanks for coming down here, Ms. Cooper. How do you like our little town? It's pretty busy right now with the fair coming up in a couple of weeks."

"I like it here. And call me Grace, please. I've met some really nice people. I'm staying at the 4-Poster. Marge is a lovely lady, so full of local lore. It piques my interest, being a magazine writer."

"A writer?" Jake replied. "How do you come up with story ideas?"

"I like people," Grace continued. "I like to look for unusual situations and find out how they came about and explain the motivation that causes people to create them in the first place. Does that make sense?"

"Yes. Perhaps we can share our information about the mystery lights. That's why you came to the Bay, you said. It sounds like an interesting profession. I'd like to talk more about that and your

39

other investigations."

Jake paused for a moment. "Listen, it's getting late. We've got a great seafood restaurant here in town, The Oyster Shack. We can talk there. It's a more comfortable place than here in the department. And since you're going to be in the Bay awhile, I'd like to get to know you better. What do you think?"

Grace looked surprised, but pleased. Sheriff Mason was actually hitting on her. Perfect. She'd have no problem with that. She was attracted to him the moment she laid eyes on him.

"Well, yes, why not?"

"It's not far from here. It's casual. Do you mind if we just walked there?"

"No, not at all."

Clyde watched as Grace and Jake left the department together. Jake glanced back at Clyde and smiled at him. Clyde just shook his head and winked at Tina.

Ten

As Jake entered The Oyster Shack, he looked back out toward Fisher Island. Dark grey clouds sat on the horizon. Long fingers of sunlight sliced through the lingering clouds. For a moment the island was illuminated and just as suddenly the light disappeared, leaving it once more shrouded in darkness.

Looking at the island and the inevitable storm ahead, he knew they'd better make it an early evening.

Once Jake was inside, the cool air and the aroma of succulent seafood cooking delighted his senses. He'd always lived by the ocean and loved the strong scent of the salty sea.

The host approached them, menus in hand and then pointed to a secluded table by the window facing the land side of the restaurant. As the host seated Grace, Jake once again was impressed with her natural beauty. Grace was dressed in a deeply cut white sleeveless sundress that exposed her smooth creamy tanned arms.

She must be more relaxed, he thought. Her hair, now released from its ponytail, framed her face and lay softly on her shoulders. When she reached up to take a menu, he noticed she wore a round silver bracelet made up of tiny inset diamonds separated by shiny silver stars.

"That's beautiful," he said.

"Oh, this used to be my mother's," Grace said, her eyes misting. "It meant a great deal to her. She never took it off, and neither do I."

Jake was happy she was there with him in that moment. He hadn't felt drawn to a woman in a long time.

The server was asking for their drink orders. Jake was somewhere else.

Grace's voice broke the spell. "Sheriff, your drink order?"

He looked up and ordered a draft beer.

"Call me Jake."

"Before we order, Jake, I just want to apologize for being so stupid to try and go out to the island without looking at a weather report or the marina booklet. I guess I'm not much of a sailor. I'm from Nebraska. Anyway, is it all right to ask about your background?"

"Sure."

As Jake started to tell her a little about his past, she found it difficult to take her eyes off of him. He stirred something inside of her she hadn't felt in a long time. Most of her male contacts were kept at a distance and romance was usually the farthest thing from her mind. For some unknown reason, she felt a connection to Jake Mason, to this man she just met. She'd have to be very careful to keep herself in check. Why did he have to be so damn appealing?

She heard him say something about the strange lights which brought her back.

"Where did you read about the lights?" he was asking her.

Just then the waiter appeared carrying their dinner orders.

"Oh, the lights. It was a small article in the *Boston Globe*. It really peaked my curiosity."

They enjoyed one another's company so much, it seemed like only moments when the waiter presented Jake with the check.

Later, as they stood in front of the 4-Poster, Grace reached out to shake Jake's hand.

"I had a lovely evening, Jake. Thanks for the invitation. I really like the restaurant. Maybe we can do this again sometime when you're not too busy."

Jake took her hand in his. "Would you like to catch a movie over in Farmsville on Wednesday evening? I don't know what's playing."

She liked the feel of his hand in hers and smiled at him. "Sure, why not. Call me."

Rain was just starting to fall. "Gotta go."

"Do you want me to get you an umbrella?"

"No, I'll be fine. My car's at the department. I think I'll make it back before it gets nasty. Talk to you soon. Better get going. 'Night!"

"'Night!" Grace called back, watching him disappear out of sight into the darkness.

Covering her head with her scarf, she ran up the stairs onto the porch. She saw Marge sitting in the parlor crocheting a lace doily. Maxie lay by her feet. Her two nieces were doing a picture puzzle on the dining room table.

"Hello, Grace. Did you enjoy your dinner?"

"Yes, very much. The food at the Shack is quite tasty. Say, you heard about the storm tonight? It's supposed to be severe."

"Oh yes, honey. We've been through a lot of these storms. It'll pass. Don't you worry about it. Tomorrow the sun'll be out. You'll see. Oh, before you go, I'd like to introduce you to my two nieces, Karen and Lucy."

"Nice to meet you girls. I'll bet you enjoy visiting your Aunt."

The girls looked up from their puzzle and smiled at Grace.

Marge beamed. "They're such a joy. Sleep well, Grace."

"Thanks. You too. Good night." And Grace climbed up the stairs. It was really quiet. No one around. But first, she had tie up some loose ends.

On his way back to the beach house, rain pelted Jake's car window. The approaching storm was moving in more quickly than predicted and appeared ominous. It was totally dark now and streaks of lightning lit up the horizon.

As soon as he let himself in, he went over to his desk calendar and penciled in *Grace, Wednesday night movie*, and then took the liberty to write in the following *Sunday, Grace, sailing date*. Why not, he thought to himself. How could she resist him? And laughed at himself. Saturday, he wanted to get in that hike up to the Ridge.

After he tied down the chairs outside and checked the windows, he fell into bed. Not even the blustery storm kept him awake. By morning, as Marge had predicted, the sun was out once more. That was the kind of weather they had each summer. They'd become used to it over the years.

Eleven

Saturday, Jake called into the station before he left the beach house, reminding Tina he was headed up to the Ridge. It would take a few hours, but he'd be back by dinner time. If he didn't make it back by five, he told her, go on home. He told her to switch all calls to his cell phone and he'd alert Clyde in case of emergency.

He kept a steady pace through the forest. When he reached the open field just below the Ridge, it was just as Clyde had described it. As he surveyed the perimeter and the field itself, he could see why Clyde was so enthusiastic.

He took out his water bottle and drank half of it.

He could just about see the house high on the hill above the path ahead. He decided to head to the far west end, where Fulmer said he had been standing when he saw the lights, and see the island from his perspective. When he reached the spot, he took out his binoculars and focused on the southern end of the island. There was nothing visible that could have emitted the pulsating lights. He wasn't surprised. He shielded his eyes and looked skyward. The sun was about in the same position as when Fulmer saw the lights, but again, there was nothing. Disappointing.

He turned around and headed back toward the

house, checking for signs of activity along the way. He made his way through the tangled weeds surrounding the grounds. When he looked up, he was impressed with what must have been a grand mansion in its day. Now it was in its final stages of decay. He was surprised Clyde could actually walk through the interior. But, that was six years ago, he thought.

He looked at his watch, 5:00. Good thing he'd made arrangements to cover the station before he left. He made a slow circle around the house, finding only a few crushed weeds as if someone had passed close to it fairly recently. Probably someone as curious as he was. He made some notes of what he'd observed so far. He ended up at the front of the house.

Jake climbed the rickety stairs and pulled a board off the window to the left of the doorway. The glass was broken behind it and what was left of it yielded easily to the butt of Jake's service revolver. A sparrow lay dead on the living room floor, having flown in through a hole above the doorway. He bent down to look through the broken window and could see place settings, left exactly as Clyde had described. He didn't want to go inside. He'd seen enough.

The sun was now low in the sky as he headed back down the path to town. He couldn't help thinking of Grace and looked forward to their being together again.

Twelve

Over the next two weeks, Jake and Grace went back to The Oyster Shack for dinner several times. He enjoyed being with her. They always seem to have fun no matter what they did together. The weather had been perfect for their sailing date. He'd taken her out to Crook Neck Island and they picnicked there near the abandoned lighthouse.

Tonight, they planned to cut the evening short and headed back to the 4-Poster early. Jake had an early meeting at the station. They were standing on the front porch as the first drops of rain fell. Grace hoped it would end before morning.

Jake moved closer to her so that they stood near enough to touch. He was thinking how beautiful she looked in the glow of the dim porch light. She moved back away from him to avoid giving in to her feelings. She knew where that would lead.

Grace took a deep breath and extended her hand.

Jake's gaze never left her beautiful green eyes. He reached over and took both her hands in his and kissed them.

"I really enjoy being with you, Grace. You know that, don't you?"

"I like you too, Jake. I've enjoyed our time together, very much," she whispered as she took her hands out of his. She leaned up and kissed him on the cheek. "Goodnight, Jake."

As she turned to leave, Jake caught her by her arm and started to pull her back toward him.

She looked up at him and said, "No, Jake. I can't, not yet."

He released her arm. "OK, it's OK."

As Jake started to leave, he stopped at the foot of the stairs and called back to her.

"Monday is the 4th of July. Would you like to go over to Farmsville with me to watch the fireworks?"

He didn't have to wait. "Sure. Love to. Talk to you soon," she answered. "Now get in your car, before you're soaked."

Back inside the Poster, the front rooms were empty, which made her happy she didn't have to make any small talk. She wanted to think about Jake and about what she had to do the next day.

When she entered her room, she checked to be sure the briefcase was lying undisturbed where she left it atop the bookcase.

She pulled her suitcase from under the bed and removed an empty backpack. She began to fill it with what she thought she'd need for the next two days. When she was done, she put the suitcase back under the bed. She took a canteen from the bureau drawer, went down the hall to the bathroom, and filled it with water. She tossed her jacket and a rain poncho over the back of the chair and placed her hiking boots underneath.

She picked up a pad of paper on the nightstand and wrote a short note to Marge. She folded it neatly and taped it to the hook holding the filigreed key hanging on the outside of the room door. Marge would find it the next day when she came up to change the flowers in the bud vase above the key hook. It asked Marge to call Jake with the message. Now for some sleep. She had a big day tomorrow.

Thirteen

The dark haired man, almost invisible in his black clothing, chose this night because the weather forecast predicted a dense cloud cover followed by a torrential downpour. When he left the base, the storm had just passed. The moon, playing hide and seek, slid behind the thick clouds, producing a luminous gold halo. Then the sky went black. The darkness disguised the small boat in the heavy waves.

The motor purred softly, moving slowly, not to attract attention from any other boater crazy enough to venture out on a night of predicted danger. He was an experienced sailor. He crossed the waves at an angle to minimize tipping over.

He could barely make out the opposite shore as the wind drove salt spray into his eyes. His heart racing with excitement, he made out the shoreline, a long stretch of rocks with only a few places to tie up a boat. The dreaded east wind tore into the weeping willow trees that lined the shore, whipping them back and forth. With all the strength he had remaining, the man headed to a spot that had been staked out some time ago. Invisible from the water, it was a perfect place to hide a boat. He maneuvered the boat in among the tall grasses beneath a stand of cascading willow trees.

A small trail wound through the woods that would lead him up Hawksview Ridge to the old Morefield House. Yes, this is exactly the place they needed. He was lucky they had found it on their third excursion to the mainland. Lucky indeed! He felt the first drops of rain returning. He'd better get the boat unloaded quickly.

Fourteen

Jake took some time to fall asleep. All he could think about was Grace. He felt like a teenager again. He had to go outside to tie down a banging shutter unhinged by the driving wind. He fumbled around in the dark, clamped his teeth around the tiny flashlight he held in his mouth, and nailed the shutter closed. By the time he got inside again, he was soaking wet. Maybe a hot shower would help him get to sleep. He liked a really hot shower, one that would turn his skin red, the heat turning up his temperature, then dropping him into a state of complete relaxation.

Just before the steam enveloped his six-three body, he could make out his image in the shiny tiles. "Hmm," he said out loud. "Not bad. Not bad for 42. Well, I still have all my hair." He raised his right arm and flexed his muscle. "OK, Grace, what do you think?" And then, he laughed.

After fifteen minutes, he stepped out of the

shower, towel-dried and slipped back under the covers.

"OK, let's give sleep another try."

Setting the clock for 6 a.m., he turned out the light. His mind slipped into a blissful haze, that place between wakefulness and sleep. The last thing he remembered was imagining Grace in his arms and how soft and sweet she felt. He hadn't been with a woman in so long.

The alarm woke Jake with a start. He dressed and headed in to work.

At the department later that afternoon, Jake stopped to talk to Tina.

"Hey," he asked. "You didn't get any messages from Grace today? I thought I'd hear from her by now. Hope she's all right. She's probably waiting for me to call her."

"Nope, have not."

"Well, I've asked her to go to Farmsville to see the fireworks Monday."

"You got it bad, huh, Chief?" Tina asked, perching on his desk.

"I like being with her. She's really interesting as well as beautiful, but I haven't been able to totally figure her out yet."

"Well, Jake, take it from a woman, you'll never be able to solve that mystery. Just go and have a good time."

"Look, I didn't mean to ask for romantic advice, you know," Jake said.

"It's good to see you getting out more, Jake,"

Tina said. "And she seems like a nice girl. Sam and Turner have already volunteered to cover on the 4th and we can call in the volunteers in an emergency until you get back here. Go and enjoy yourself."

"Thanks, Tina. Woman or not, I will solve that mystery. The detective inside me can't see it any other way."

"Good luck, Chief."

"Say, could you get Marge Forstrum on the phone. Find out if Grace is in the house."

A few moments later Tina appeared in Jake's doorway. "Hey Chief, Marge said Grace had left a note she'd be out of town for a couple of days and if you called, she'd see you Monday."

"Thanks, Tina."

Why didn't she mention that when they got back to the Poster last night? Where could she possibly be going, he wondered.

Fifteen

Grace tried to get in a few hours of sleep before she left in the early morning before dawn. She wanted to dream about Jake. She started to get excited just thinking about him. This worried her. This wasn't part of the plan, but she found herself looking forward to seeing him again on the 4th. Settle down, she told herself.

At 3 a.m., Grace dressed, tightened the backpack straps on her shoulders and scanned the room. Did she have everything she needed? As soon as she quietly closed her door, Maxie was by her side, greeting her with a soft "woof." She patted his head and put her finger to her lips, as if the dog could understand the meaning of the gesture.

He trotted behind her, only stopping when she left the Poster through the door leading to the garden and out the back gate. She looked back and could see him wagging his tail in the garden doorway. She liked him. She missed having a dog. Much to her relief the rain had let up. But the path was muddied and slippery. She had to be careful.

She made her way in the darkness using a small flashlight, arcing it back and forth in front of her. She found the path that started south of the Greyston Farm. It switchbacked its way up the hill through the wild blueberry patches until it reached the rocky cliffs overlooking Caswell Bay. She paused briefly, looking down on the small cabins circled below. The Bide a Wee cabins should be filled by now, even the ones at the top of the hill back in the trees. She swung the flashlight ahead of her, searching out a small opening in the scrub brush. She heard a door open and close down below to her right and a dog bark. She switched off her flashlight. It sounded like a man's voice shushing the dog. Then the sound of the door opening and closing again, and all was quiet once more.

She made her way down the steep rocky path until she was in sight of a darkened cabin. Looking both ways she made her way to the front and could see a wood sign nailed to the front porch overhang. A quick on and off of her flashlight revealed a large number 15. She headed to her right, counting each cabin as she passed by. The third should be the one. The beam on her flashlight illuminated number 18. Yes, she thought. Grace looked forward to lying down for a while. She wasn't supposed to leave until 4 p.m.

She reached under the welcome mat and found the key just where it was supposed to be. Upon entering the cabin, she was careful to close the door softly. She didn't turn on any lights. Grace hung the "do not disturb" sign on the front door and lay down on one of the twin beds. It had another bedroom, a bathroom, and fortunately a kitchen as well.

She hoped that most of the people would be out of the area by the time she had to leave. As soon as she closed her eyes, she thought of Jake again. Was he thinking of her as well? She really liked him.

Her thoughts shifted to the day ahead. Grace felt ready. She'd been in tough situations before; she could handle this one. She pulled her cell phone out of her backpack and put it on the nightstand. She then pulled out a loaded .38 and put it under the bed within easy reach. Grace lay back down again and closed her eyes. She realized that she was slowly turning her starry silver bracelet round and round on her wrist. That usually happened when she was trying to make an important decision. Everything will be fine, she thought. Grace wrapped her blanket tighter around her, and fell asleep.

Sixteen

The sound of a horn awakened Grace and she sat bolt upright. Was it part of the dream she was having? No. Then came the reality of where she was in the moment. She moved quickly to the window and peeked out between the closed curtains. She could see an old Chevy pickup with a bicycle in the rear bed bumping its way over the rutted road toward town. There seemed to be no other activity.

She looked at her watch, 3 p.m. The cabin had been stocked with supplies and even had food and water in the fridge. Great. She fixed herself a ham and cheese sandwich. Grace sat at the table and looked at a map in front of her. Then she went into the bedroom and picked up her phone. Time to check in.

By 4 p.m., she was packed and ready to go. She tucked her ponytail under her cap and put on sunglasses. Looking both ways for signs of life and finding none, she removed the "do not disturb" sign, locked the door and replaced the key under the mat. The path was uphill now, but easier to maneuver because she could see where she was going. The sun had dried up most of the mud. She could see the start of the evergreen forest ahead of her. Still no one in sight. So far, so good.

Two hours later, the forest began to thicken and close in around her. The bay had disappeared and darkness wrapped around her like an unwelcome blanket. She sat down on a rock and rechecked the map. Yes, she was on the right path. She pulled out a candy bar and drank some water. Hearing the chirping sounds of birds high above made her feel less alone. She wanted to get to the Ridge before dark.

She still had Boulder Hill to climb over and she was getting tired. An hour later when she saw the boulders ahead, she gave a sigh of relief. According to her map, the open meadow would be a half hour away and the Ridge another twenty minutes. She should reach the Morefield House by 8 p.m. And then what?

Seventeen

Dimitri sat on the last step of the crumbling staircase leading up to the porch smoking a cigarette. He inhaled deeply and felt free to be out in the open, his claustrophobia gone for the moment. He didn't look forward to having to return to his cramped quarters tomorrow evening, but he had no choice. He was bored with this assignment. He was usually sent to places that needed his special skills. He still wondered who Vorack would target for removal.

He also wondered if all the buildup for Grace Cooper, was warranted. She must be good at what she does, or that maniac Major wouldn't be so anxious to have her join them. He looked at his watch. She should be arriving soon. He ground out his cigarette, walked over to the path leading to the meadow and looked through his binoculars. Well, what do you know, he thought. She made it. OK, lady. Let's see what you can do. He couldn't wait to introduce her to the Major. Hope she has a strong will. She's going to need it.

Grace crested the hill and saw the decaying Morefield House in front of her. The peeling siding, grey with age, now allowed only the imagination to describe the grandeur of its youth. Fallen branches, leaves and green moss covered the roof. A small maple tree sapling was growing out of the gutter overhanging the front porch. Grace wished she could have seen it in its day. As she moved through the rusted iron gateway, now partly tilted on its side, she saw a man wearing a baseball cap walking toward her. He had a rifle slung over one shoulder. She felt uncomfortable right away. She was tired; her reflexes wouldn't be as sharp if it came to a confrontation. She kept her hand on the loaded pistol in her pocket.

"Grace Cooper?"

"Yes."

"Good. Just call me Dimitri. That's a long trip isn't it. I'll answer any questions you have when we get inside. Follow me." He headed back toward the house. "Oh, be careful where you walk. Disturb as little as possible. Follow in my tracks."

"Right, will do."

As they crossed the yard toward the back of the house, she noticed the wildflowers and tall grasses showed little sign of breakage except where they walked and a few growing near the front porch. Thick tangled rose bushes pressed up against the west side of the house and crept over the broken storm cellar door partially buried, loosely covered with soil in the backyard. Under the vines, the door was held together by a long grey weathered wood plank someone had long ago nailed across its entrance.

Her eyes shifted to the upstairs. The windows looked mainly intact except for two on what she assumed was the attic level. There was a large jagged hole next to a shutter which had fallen to one side, ready to complete its decay in the next windstorm.

"For an old place, they don't have many trees," Grace remarked to Dimitri.

"There used to be tall trees, elms, I think they were called. They got some disease and died. Now, see, just short trees; maples and oaks I think. It's a wonder the house is here at all. We were lucky to find such a place. No one comes here. Just what we needed."

He didn't want to tell her that someone had been snooping around a couple of weeks earlier and broke a window in the front of the house. Whoever it was didn't come inside, lucky for all of them. Must have been somebody passing by, just curiosity. They've been on guard ever since.

As they entered through the back door, Grace was taken aback.

"Something else, no?"

She couldn't speak for a moment. "Wow, unbelievable. What happened here? Look at all this. Look in the hutch at those beautiful decorated plates. I'll bet they're Limoges. The tea has to be Bavarian. These are very valuable. How could they be left here like this? It's like a museum that time forgot."

"Who knows?" was Dimitri's unemotional response. "It's weird. Don't touch anything. We work downstairs. Come."

Grace became aware of a low whining noise,

63

very much out of place in a house supposedly empty of life. The noise became louder as she neared the bottom of the stairs.

"We're back," called out Dimitri.

Two men and a woman were already on their feet.

One said something in an angry voice in Russian. Dimitri waggled a finger at him "English only, Maxim. I'll tell the Major on you."

The woman laughed. "It's a great pleasure to work with such a funny guy, Dimitri. Just don't scare us again." She returned her pistol to the drawer in the work table in front of her.

"Natasia, I'd like you to meet our new cipher genius, Grace Cooper."

"Good to meet you," she replied. "We can use a genius right now."

The third man was already extending his hand to Grace. "Sergei at your service pretty lady."

"You must watch out for him, Grace," chided Natasia.

"Good to meet you all. Now how can I help here?"

"OK, all of you, back to work. I have to talk with Grace."

Dimitri took Grace over to a small green table that had seen better days, like everything else in the house. They sat facing each other and Dimitri opened an envelope which looked like the one she'd received earlier. It must be from Major Vorack she thought.

While Dimitri was going through the papers, she scanned the room. The three Russians were busy addressing whatever was scrolling down their computer screens. Their work benches looked almost new. More benches wrapped around the walls on either side of them. Above them, shelving held manuals and other books. A printer sat in one corner. She couldn't tell where the source of electricity was located.

She looked over her shoulder and saw another room with a large open doorway. She could make out bunks where they slept and what looked like a makeshift shower in the corner. A large bucket of water sat on the floor next to it. She didn't see any bathroom. Her inventory was interrupted by Dimitri.

"Grace, look at me. You can go exploring later. You have a packet from the Major, I know, with your instructions so far. You've connected with us by phone, using the correct password. You've checked with the locals about the lights. The Major is very pleased with your progress. He said to tell you he's also very pleased that you've been in contact with Sheriff Mason. From all reports, he feels that's going very well." Dimitri looked her in the eyes and smiled broadly.

"Do you have someone spying on me, Dimitri?" she asked, her voice raising in anger.

"The Major has eyes everywhere. He never leaves anything or anyone to chance. Better get used to it. We have several agents that float around town. Don't try to find any of them. You won't. Anyway, don't worry. They can help out too in an emergency."

Grace was about to reply, but Dmitri talked over her.

"The Major wanted me to remind you that we need to be kept informed as to what the Sheriff's

Department knows. You can call that number any time of day, give the correct password, and someone will take the message."

"OK," he continued. "You've been brought up here because this is our communications center. Someone's always here night and day. We receive all transmissions. Fisher Island is our base of operations and that's where the Major runs the other parts of the mission. Transmission under so much rock is spotty, that's why we use this house. We send out and receive communications that the Major can't. We can see and usually can communicate with the island and keep a watch on the sea lanes, which will be even more important shortly. Very importantly—"

Grace interrupted, "Did you say Fisher Island? Where on earth is this base of operations located? That seems impossible."

"OK, Grace. I'll explain more about that. Be patient. In fact, I'm going to take you out there to meet our illustrious Major. Now for the moment, just listen. The three people you see at their computers are extremely proficient, but we have two problems we need your help with. The first is, there's a transmission from, let's call him a client, of the Major's that we cannot open. The encryption is unknown. The second is equally important. We have information that the FBI is trying to find the Major and shut down his operation."

"How do you know that?" asked Grace.

"The Major told me that we have one of our people embedded in the FBI. I don't know who it is, but this person has been in contact with someone high up in the KGB. We understand that the FBI has

66

been looking for the Major for some time and is close to finding him. We want to know what the FBI knows."

"We're close to ending this mission, Grace, which will, of course, allow the Major to once more disappear until needed again by our government. We understand that the FBI believes the Major is in this area and will be setting up surveillance somewhere on the outskirts of town shortly. We want to be able to monitor their communications. Do you think you can accomplish these tasks?"

"Well, Dimitri, this isn't going to be easy. The encryption translation should not be a problem, but until the FBI is actually in the area, even when they're here, I just don't know."

"We'll see how the Major feels about your response. We're going out to the island tomorrow night to meet with him. Perhaps you'll have the encryption solved by that time at least."

"Look, Dimitri. I've got to be back in town for the 4th. I'm supposed to meet with Jake, Sheriff Mason."

"Don't worry. I'll see you get back on time."

That night, as Grace tried to fall asleep, she heard a low moaning sound. It wouldn't stop. She felt the hair on her arms start to stand up. Raising up on her elbows, she looked across the room at Natasia who lay on her back snuffling softly. She threw back the covers and crossed the room and gently nudged Dimitri, who woke with a start.

"What are you doing?" he stared up at her.

Grace put her fingers to her lips. "Listen. Do you

hear that?"

"Oh, that," he said letting out a deep breath from his lungs, "Don't worry. It's just the wind blowing in through a cracked window in the attic. It's creepy here. I don't believe in ghosts. We just need to cover up the window, but never seem to get around to it. It's easier to wear ear plugs. I promise to fix it in the morning. Go back and try to sleep. We'll be out of here soon."

But the sound disturbed her. She lay back down and pulled the blanket over her head. The moaning noise took her back to her childhood when there was little to eat and her mother would cry herself to sleep. After her mother died, she lived with her grandparents who cared for her and gave her the opportunity to go to college. Whenever she heard that sound, she's right back there with her mother. She pulled the covers up tightly around her ears and finally drifted off.

Eighteen

Early the next evening, Dimitri stood on the edge of the cliff outside the house, staring through a pair of high powered binoculars. He waited for the signal as he'd done in the past. Grace followed his gaze across the water toward Fisher Island.

A sequence of lights emanated from the south end of the island; red, blue, and then two reds. Grace watched fascinated. Jake would be astounded that she solved the mystery of the odd flashing lights. She wished she could tell him.

"OK, Grace, let's get started," Dimitri said. "It won't take as long to Pickett's Point as it did for you to get up here from the cabin. I know a shortcut. Just follow me and stay close. We should be there in about an hour and a half."

When they reached the Point, he told her to stop and wait. Dimitri moved toward a rock jutting out of the water. He stopped and took a long black cylinder out of his backpack. It looked like an oversized flashlight. Aiming it at the island, he sent a light signal to the island. Grace couldn't see the color code he used, but saw the return signal, now two blues and one red.

He made his way back to her and began the trip down from the Ridge through a thicket of tangled weeds and back through the forest for a short time. Eventually the rarely used path led to an opening where a small motor boat was tied up. It was just where Dimitri left it in the tall sea grasses.

The sun had just set and activity had ceased in the harbor. It took fifteen minutes to cross through the calm waters and reach the south end of the island. Dimitri kept the boat close to the shoreline. He knew the waters well by now, having made this trip several times in the past. Avoiding the submerged rocks had been tricky.

As they passed between the lighthouse and the rocky shore, the island's western side became visible. In the last glow of the setting sun, Grace made out the blanket of algae floating on the surface of the water up ahead. It started to clump around the boat and the motor sputtered.

Dimitri slowed their forward momentum and handed her a paddle. "Sit up front and try to push the algae aside," he snapped. "We're almost there." Grace looked around and couldn't figure out where "there" was. She saw nothing, no sign of life. The sharp cliffs devoid of plants loomed above her. The algae slapped against the hull of the boat. The cool breeze made her shiver under the light jacket she was wearing.

They were two thirds of the way around the

island and Dimitri turned sharply and headed the boat straight in toward the island. Grace, caught off guard, almost dropped the paddle into the water.

Dimitri shifted the boat into idle and stood up, once again sending a short signal from the cylinder toward the rocky promontory in front of him. Suddenly, the embankment ahead of them slowly slid to one side revealing a dark passage. He moved the boat ahead and slipped inside. The door, still dripping with sea water and algae, slid shut behind them.

Very impressive, Grace thought. How did they ever manage to pull this off without anyone's knowledge? It had to have taken a very long time. She had lots of questions to ask, but doubted she'd get all the answers.

She noticed the short narrow passage had a walkway on either side and ended a few feet ahead. Once more the passage slid open in front of them and a wide light-filled docking room became visible. Men in blue jumpsuits scurried around the dock stacking what looked like waterproofed boxes against the far wall.

As they pulled their boat up against the dock, a hand reached down to help Grace out of the boat. As she looked up, she recognized Major Anton Vorack right away. No mistaking him. He appeared older than his photos, wearier, she thought. His eyes were cold; like a falcon sizing up its prey.

"Welcome," Vorack intoned. "We hope you'll like your new home."

Grace felt claustrophobic. No way could she think of this place as home. She looked over at Dimitri.

Dimitri smiled. "Indeed, welcome home, Grace."

He climbed up on the dock and followed the Major and Grace down a hallway and up the stairs to the Major's office. On their way up the stairs, they were joined by another man who was tall, muscular, and bald. He walked closely behind them, as if to prevent their change in direction.

Dimitri looked back over his shoulder. "Well, hello Karl. So good you could join us."

He didn't like this apelike bodyguard of the Major's. He didn't trust him for a moment.

Ushered into the Major's office, Vorack told them, "Sit, sit, both of you. Grace, I wanted to meet you face to face. You were able to become quite friendly with our Sheriff, Jake Mason. You were observed at dinner with him. Anything new to report?"

"He only talked a little about himself, but told me we'd work together finding out about the flashing light signals."

"I hope you are right, my dear. As you know, being aware of the Sheriff's Department activity is very important. And I understand, you've been informed the FBI will soon be interfering with our plans if we aren't careful. Dimitri tells me, Grace, that you seem to be reluctant to move forward with breaking into their communications, hacking, you call it. And why is that?"

"No, no Major. He misunderstood. What I told him was that I couldn't do anything until they were in the area."

"I still don't understand, Grace. Why do you have to wait?"

Grace tried not to seem evasive, but make him

understand it would be easier to isolate the messages, to be sure they were talking about him. Their messages would undoubtedly be coded. She told him that this was her field of expertise. And then she made the mistake of telling him to be patient.

"Patient?" he roared. "Now you listen to me. We don't have time to be patient." He started around his desk and loomed over her, his hand raised about to strike. "Summerfair is my target date and it's—"

Grace scrambled backward in her chair away from him, trying to fend off the inevitable blow. She almost fell backwards.

Vorack suddenly stopped and lowered his hand. He reached forward and pulled her chair back into an upright position. She had an important job to do for him, he thought, and he needed her full cooperation. He'd take care of her later.

"Now that's no way to begin our relationship Ms. Cooper," he said, modulating his voice. "Since you don't know about our mission, you couldn't understand that this is a very tense moment for me. It will be completed soon and with your full cooperation. I will tell you the details of the mission at another time. Please accept my apology."

Grace resumed her composure and now sat bolt upright in her chair. She stared directly into his eyes. She'd suddenly learned a lot about this Major Vorack. He was as dangerous as he'd been described. She'd been told about his unpredictable behavior. She was ready for him now.

"Of course, Major," she answered in the coldest voice she could muster.

Dimitri was stunned. He'd never heard the Major

apologize to anyone before. Usually he just sent them somewhere to be tortured or killed. He thought that Grace had to be important to him. But how?

Vorack opened the door and spoke to Karl standing guard outside.

"Grace, Karl will give you a tour of our facility. Dimitri, you stay here. I want to talk to you."

Grace looked back at Dimitri as she exited with Karl. Vorack stood behind his desk looking for something on the table top. Dimitri looked back at Grace and nodded. She seemed to have gotten through her first round with the maniac.

Vorack walked over and closed the door.

"Dimitri, soon I will I want you to do something for me, something that will appeal to your special talents."

Nineteen

The next day, Grace casually made her way through the facility. She was always aware of being watched by the surveillance cameras. She discovered that if she stood below the camera and to the right, there was a small blind spot. She'd observed it on her tour with Karl the night before when they entered the security area. That room had given her the most information. She scanned the bank of monitors and observed men in white coats working on something. She didn't have time to make out what it was.

Others were grouped around a table with what looked like schematic drawings of some sort of instrument. Karl called her before she had a good look at it. When they left the area, she caught a glance at one of the monitors displaying what looked like a large metal door somewhat like a wall-sized safe. An armed guard stood in front of the entrance.

Later in the day, as she entered the cafeteria, she saw some of the same white-coated men, obviously scientists or engineers. From where she sat eating her chicken salad sandwich, she thought they looked to be Russian. Two were definitely oriental, probably Chinese. She couldn't hear what they were saying. But when one left the table, he said he'd see the others later. His English was very good.

In the middle of her casual surveillance, Dimitri came over carrying a hot dog and a can of cola.

"Well, Dimitri, that really looks nourishing."

"Hey, we're in America. I like the food. I haven't seen you since you met our exalted leader. Great guy, huh?" He laughed. "You did good. You've gotta be careful, you know. People can disappear easily and no one asks why."

"I'll be OK. I know it's important to not, as you say, rattle his chain."

"How did you like your tour with Karl?" Dimitri continued. "It's quite a place, isn't it? It's amazing they were able to carve it out of rock and have it hold together."

"You're right about that, but it'll make me happy to get back on dry land. Listen, I wanted to ask you. I noticed that unless you're a guard here—and there sure are a lot of them—who are all these white coated men and women?"

"Well, Grace, I suspect they're scientists," Dimitri said with a shrug. "I heard they were working on some top-secret invention, but no one talks about it. You can't pry it out of them. I've watched. Their labs have coded keyboards. When the door shuts, you can hear it lock automatically. They have their own sleeping sections and only show up once in a while here in the cafeteria. Maybe, they have their own eating sections too. I'm as curious as you are about them. Oh yes, I have an important message from the Major. He expects you back at the house in two days with the FBI information. Don't fuck up, as the Americans are fond of saying."

"Listen, Dimitri. How does he expect me to get the information he wants from the sheriff and be working at the Morefield House at the same time?"

"That's part of his charm, Grace. I thought you learned by now, what Vorack wants, he gets—or else. See you later, Grace, and good luck."

Twenty

When they arrived back at Pickett's Point, Dimitri returned the boat to its hiding place. He went back up to the Morefield House after sending Grace on a different path toward town, bypassing the cabins where she'd started out two days earlier.

Grace made her way back to the 4-Poster. She returned through the garden gate, looking up to see Maxie in the doorway. She laughed to herself, pretending he missed her so much that he'd been sitting there ever since she left two days earlier. He licked her hand when she patted his head and he followed her up the deserted darkened staircase to her room door.

After she closed the door, Grace heard him lay down outside the door. That pleased her very much. The loving thoughts she recaptured by encountering this sweet dog made her think of the good things in life. She tried to put the events of the house and the island out of her mind as she undressed.

Soon she lay completely relaxed under the soft comforter that covered her bed. She thought of Jake. Grace wondered why there wasn't a woman in his life. Maybe, he was waiting for her. She smiled at the thought. Yes, she was really looking forward to seeing him tomorrow afternoon, but not as a spy trying to get information out of him. Well, that's what she was, a spy. Closing her eyes, she relived their last meeting and how close she was to letting him hold her and kiss her goodnight. She knew he wanted her as much as she wanted him. She couldn't hold out much longer.

Twenty-one

As Grace left for a late breakfast the next morning, she noticed her little door vase was filled with tiny purple violets and lilies of the valley. She stopped to inhale their sweet aroma. It was late. She was probably the last one to arrive and hoped there'd still be blueberry pancakes waiting for her. Marge was a great cook. She had a helper, Betty, when times were busy, but did most of the work herself. Turning around, Grace almost ran head long into Marge's niece, Lucy.

"Whoa, sorry," she apologized. "Lucy. Where are you going so fast?"

"Sorry to run into you. I'm in a hurry. Auntie Marge is going to teach me how to make gingerbread men." And off she ran.

"Save me a cookie," Grace called in her wake. Lucy was such a pretty little girl—so full of energy and promise. She wondered what it would be like to have a daughter, a husband, or any family that stayed in one place for any length of time. She wondered if she'd ever have that opportunity.

As she expected, no one was at the breakfast table, but a place was left set for her and wasn't that nice, she thought. Just then Marge came out of the kitchen double doors, her hands covered in gingerbread dough.

"Good morning, Grace," she said. "Happy to see you back safely from wherever you went."

The two leaned awkwardly toward each other, maneuvering to avoid Marge smearing Grace with flour.

"Where did you go anyway?" Grace asked. "Jake was worried about you just taking off like that. Good thing you left a note. He might have sent out the cavalry to find you."

"Oh, I was just over in Farmsville, checking out some information for an article I'm writing for a magazine back in Boston."

"You'll have to tell me more about that later, dear. I'm in the middle of gingerbread men baking with the girls. Betty will fix you something to eat. What would you like?"

"Do you have any blueberry pancakes left over?"

"No problem. Help yourself to coffee over there on the sideboard." Then Marge disappeared back through the double doors.

Ten minutes later, Grace was almost finished with her coffee when she looked up to see Jake standing at the end of the table.

"Wow," she said. "Good morning. I didn't expect to see you here. What a surprise. Come and sit down. I'll get you some coffee."

"I can't stay. I just came over to see if you came back. I hadn't heard from you. Are we still on for later this afternoon?"

"You bet." She felt herself blush. What a teenager you are, Grace, she thought. "Why didn't you call and save yourself the trip over?"

"I guess I just wanted to see you in person."

Grace felt herself blushing again. What is wrong with you, Grace? Stop that, she thought.

"Well, here I am," she said awkwardly.

"Yes indeed," he said smiling at her. He wanted to lift her out of her chair and—but instead said, "How about I drive over here and pick you up say about 5:00 ? By the time we get over to Farmsville, we'll have time to walk around the fair and pick up something to eat before the fireworks."

"Sounds perfect."

And, he was gone as fast as he arrived. Just then Betty came out of the kitchen with a plate of hot pancakes. Grace forgot about the last two days and how they could change her life. Right now she felt as if she'd died and gone to heaven.

Twenty-two

Promptly at 5:00, Jake pulled up in front of the 4-Poster in his 1985 red Mustang convertible with with the top down. Grace, seated in the porch swing, watched him get out and come over to the foot of the stairs.

"Aren't we the sporty one," she called down.

"Well, I do have a life away from the department," he said. "I'm even wearing civilian clothes. See what you've done to me."

"OK, Jake. This should be a fun evening."

"Count on it," he smiled and opened the car door for her. "Hope you brought a scarf."

As they drove along Main Street, Grace noticed the street lamps were festooned with red, white, and blue streamers in honor of the holiday. They'll probably remain up for the Summerfair opening in ten days, she thought. The streets were filled with holiday vacationers using up all available parking spots. The businesses were undoubtedly happy with the influx of people and knew it'd continue on through Summerfair.

The traffic lightened up outside of town. Jake called over to Grace. "Would you like to talk or listen to some music?"

"How about music right now, something Nat King Cole-ish?" Grace said. She just wanted to savor the moment.

The highway ran parallel to the ocean at times. The beaches were full and the annual 4th of July sailboat race from Pickett's Point to Clarkson Township Marina was just starting. There was a great rivalry between Clarkson and Bay Township, both vying for a trophy given out by the Yacht Club in Bath. Bay had won three years in a row.

As they approached Farmsville, the traffic slowed to almost a stop. Most people were headed for the fairgrounds. Grace could see the outline of a tall Ferris wheel in the distance.

"Almost there," Jake called over.

Close to the site, local deputies were monitoring traffic and directing people to less congested roads for parking. Jake waved at one of the men.

"Hi, Stan. How did you pull this duty?"

"Hi, Jake. Luck of the draw. Listen, I heard there are some empty spots over on Cutter Lake Road." He stepped in front of the car, held up his hand to stop traffic, and motioned Jake to turn left. "See ya."

"Well now, wasn't he nice?" Grace responded. She started pointing frantically to an open space on the right just ahead. "Quick, up there."

As they reached the midway, it teemed with people carrying popcorn, ice cream and tired children. Jake grabbed Grace's hand and pulled her over to one of the booths.

"You're empty-handed. You need a souvenir."

In back of the booth a young boy sat up high in a caged tower. A paddle extended out below the cage. An accurate hit of a pitched baseball opened the bottom of the cage, sending the boy into a deep tub of water.

"Dunk the boy and win a toy," the barker brayed. "Bring your sweetie over here and show her what you've got. Three balls for 50 cents. Who's game?"

He looked over at Jake. "How about you mister? Want to impress the pretty lady?"

Jake looked at Grace. "Well, how about it?"

"Go for it," she said, her eyes flashing. "Better not miss."

Jake threw the first ball. It hit the paddle and bounced back off. The kid laughed and taunted Jake. "Hey, mister, even my kid sister can do better than that."

Grace just shook her head. The second ball hit the corner of the cage. Grace bent over laughing; the kid continued to taunt Jake. Jake turned around and looked Grace in the eye.

"This one has your name on it," he said and wound up to throw. The ball hit the paddle so hard it swung backward and almost flew off its hinges. The surprised boy hit the water like a ton of bricks. Water splashed out of the tub and almost soaked Jake twenty feet away.

"Wow," the barker said. "Are you some professional ball player?"

Grace ran over and flung her arms around Jake's neck, almost knocking him over.

"That was amazing. Thank you."

"No, wow, thank you," he said, and hugged her back with equal bravado.

"Pick anything," the barker told Grace as a soggy kid, towel in hand, grudgingly climbed back inside the cage.

"Nice going mister," he called over to Jake who was still enjoying Grace's body next to his.

She pulled herself away and pointed at a stuffed brown shepherd dog on the top shelf. He reminded her of Maxie.

"Good choice," Jake said sizing up the dog as he held it at arm's length before handing it to her. "Bet you picked it because it looks a little like Maxie."

"Well, aren't you a mind reader," she said with a laugh. Grace tucked the dog under her arm and continued walking down the fairway, her body as close to Jake's as possible without touching him.

They went on a few rides and stopped into an outdoor re-creation of a German beer garden, where they decided to have dinner. Grace asked Jake to tell her more about himself.

"What brought you to this little town of Caswell Bay?" Grace asked. "I understand you were a police lieutenant in LA. This must be quite a change." She wanted to keep the conversation light and learn more about him, but with her question, Jake grew solemn.

"I came here to be with my father," Jake said, his eyes misty. "He, well, he was dying and I had to be with him."

"Oh Jake, I'm so sorry," Grace said.

"We'd lived here together only a few months. When I came home from work one night, the neighbor's dog was on the porch pawing the front door. Dad liked Rex and gave him treats every day. I patted him on the head and went inside and called out to Dad. He didn't answer. The house seemed too quiet. I found him in his bedroom. His eyes were closed. He looked so peaceful lying there on his bed."

Grace's hand on Jake's and the look in her green eyes made him open up about things he'd buried.

"I went over to him and bent down and kissed him on the forehead," Jake continued. "I checked his pulse. I don't know how long he'd been gone. I just pulled up a chair and sat down by the bedside. I took his hand in mine. He was so cold. I don't know why, but I pulled the blanket up around him as if it would warm him. I don't know, I just sat there for what seemed like an eternity, wondering how I would get along without him."

She felt as if she were there in the room with him, as Jake told what he saw.

"Then a strange thing happened. As I got up to turn on the lamp next to the bed, the last ray of sunset caught the corner of one of my Mom's glass figurines. As it penetrated the little bird in flight, a tiny rainbow of light reflected onto the wall above the bed. I wanted to think that Mom and Dad were together again."

Grace moved over next to Jake on his side of the booth and put her arm around him as tears started down her cheeks.

"I told him to rest in peace. I miss him so." Jake choked back a sob as he buried his face in her sweet-smelling hair.

The waitress cleared her throat as she interrupted, stepping up to the table and presenting them with the bill.

As Jake and Grace left, she walked over to her co-worker "Did you see that? She was wiping away tears. They looked so sad. I wonder what happened."

Later as it started to get dark, Jake thought about going back to the car and getting a blanket to lie on up on the hillside and watch the fireworks. Seeing the Ferris wheel covered in twinkling lights looming overhead, changed his mind.

"Hey. Look up. Now that's the best place to see the fireworks. Come on," and grabbed Grace by the hand.

"Great idea, Jake. Slow down."

Stepping up to the ticket booth, he bought several strips of tickets and around and around they went for the next half hour.

As the Ferris wheel reached the top of the ride, Grace leaned over and said, "You were right. The view is spectacular from here."

She could feel the warmth of his body pressing against hers. He slid his arm around her shoulders, supposedly protecting her from the cool breeze that enwrapped them. His closeness made her feel excited, yet safe all at the same time.

She felt an intimacy with a man that she hadn't felt in a long time. She couldn't hold back any longer. She needed this. She needed Jake. He was not only physically desirable, but a genuinely nice person as well. Diverting her gaze from the fireworks, her eyes moved slowly over Jake's face, hoping he would turn around.

As if reading her mind, he did turn around and

saw her gazing up at him. He took his hand and gently pulled her face toward his and kissed her on the lips. She knew nothing else, only Jake's lips, and kissed him back with even more passion.

She pulled back at last and took a deep breath. "I wanted you to do that. It's been so much fun being with you today and now feeling you so close to me."

Just then, the Ferris wheel stopped "OK, folks, out you go. Thanks for coming."

Jake and Grace looked surprised.

"C'mon, you two love birds," he said with a grin. "Other people are waiting to ride."

The fireworks had ended and a long line of people stared expectantly at the two of them.

Grace blushed. Jake took her by the hand as they walked away.

"Let's go. We can go back to my place," Jake began. "Or we can wait if you want. I'm a patient man. Just tell me what you want."

This connection with Jake was what Grace wanted, but something told her to pull back for right now; she had to stay focused. She reached up and kissed him on the lips. "Just so you don't think I'm easy, I'll take a rain check for tonight."

Jake was disappointed. He tried to be understanding, but it wasn't easy. He didn't know if he was drawn to Grace by just pure physical attraction or because he knew that the relationship could lead to something more.

He didn't really know a lot about her, he reminded himself. They'd only known each other a short time. But there was something about Grace, something he couldn't explain. Jake couldn't wait to see her again.

Twenty-three

Grace lay down on her bed in the dark with only the street lamp's dim light filtering in through the lace curtains. She tried to work out in her mind how she could continue with both Jake and the mission. She went over several scenarios in her mind. She tossed and turned, unable to sleep. The buzzing of her vibrating phone brought her back to the present. She pulled it out of the charger on the nightstand and spoke softly; the walls were thin.

The conversation went back and forth.

"Why are you calling me now? What? Tomorrow? Yes, Dimitri, I have the message. I'll see you there about 7 p.m."

She lay back on the bed still holding the phone clasped against her chest. Dimitri said the Major wanted her back up at the Morefield House as soon as possible. Of course, to him that meant right now. She complained about having to go back so soon, but it meant nothing to Dimitri. Get over it, get up here, he had told her. Dimitri informed her that Vorack had received word from his FBI mole that the Feds would be arriving tomorrow and setting up an encampment of trailers somewhere north of the town. She was surprised the FBI hadn't found the mole yet.

She guessed that answered some questions concerning Jake and their relationship. There may not be any. She'd call him this time, though, and try to meet him for lunch at the diner. She would tell him she was headed out on another lead for her story. Then, she'd head back up to the Morefield House. She could use Dimitri's new directions. It'd save her some time. There were so many people in town now, it would be safer. Fortunately, a long hike was not in the average vacationer's itinerary. The phone, still clasped in her hands, vibrated again.

"Yes," she said angrily into the receiver. Then her voice softened. "Yes, the FBI's presence is known. No, I don't think so. I know there's a mole in the FBI. I told Dimitri I'd be at the House tonight at 7. There's a lot of work to be done. I'll stay in touch."

This time she shoved the phone deep into her backpack under the bed and covered her head with her comforter. No more calls. She really needed to get some rest. The day had drained her emotionally. Tomorrow she'd need her physical strength as well.

Twenty-four

"Good morning, Tina," Jake said as he stuck his head inside her doorway.

"Well, someone's in a good mood today. I don't need to ask how your date with Grace went. Want to share any details?"

"I'll just say we had a great time. What's happening here?"

"There's a private message for you on your desk. I think you'd better read it right away. Hope it doesn't spoil your mood."

"That sounds ominous," Jake shot back as he headed for his office.

He looked at the stack of messages on his desk. The top one had urgent written across the top, underlined, with an exclamation point. Tina wanted to be certain of its priority. Must be serious.

The message had an 800 number and only said call immediately.

Jake dialed the number.

"Federal Bureau of Investigation, Central Office. How may I direct your call?"

"My name is Sheriff Jake Mason from Caswell Bay, Maine. I received an urgent call from someone this morning, but no name was left as a contact."

"One moment, please," came the robotic reply.

"SpecialAgent Dorothy Quinn," a voice said. "Thank you for returning my call, Sheriff Mason. You need to know we have a team of agents moving into your area and want to meet with you concerning their assignment and how it will affect you and your town. I'll be flying into Portland early this morning and will be joining them as soon as possible. Could we meet in your office, say, 3:00 this afternoon?"

"Just a moment, Agent Quinn, this is the first time we've been told of any FBI presence in Caswell Bay. Just where are you going to be in our area and why are we just learning about this now?" Jake responded. "I'm not aware of anything serious happening here that would warrant a visit from the FBI. Can you fill me in on that?"

"I'm sorry if you weren't advised, but this is a very top secret assignment, which I'll be happy to discuss with you when I arrive," Quinn said. "We'll not be set up inside your town limits. I can tell you that much. If you don't mind, I'd rather wait until we can sit down together and go over the evidence we've collected so far. I'm concerned that your phones may be tapped."

"That's surprising, to say the least. I don't see how that's possible, but we'll certainly check that out asap," Jake replied. As he talked, he walked over to the door and motioned Clyde to come into the office.

"I'm more than anxious to hear your story, Agent Quinn. We'll be here waiting at three."

"I appreciate your cooperation, Sheriff Mason. See you later."

As Jake hung up, Clyde entered the office. "Come in Clyde, come in, sit. I'm going to get Tina. Be right back."

"Well, Tina, you were right about the importance of that call," Jake told her on the way back to his office. "Come on in and have a seat. It seems the FBI are coming to shake up our little town and the timing couldn't be worse with Summerfair eight days away." Jake began while pacing back and forth.

"Why?"

"I don't know yet, Clyde. She didn't want to talk over the phone. She said she thought our phones may be tapped."

"You've got to be kidding me."

"They've arranged a meeting for this afternoon at 3:00. I'd like the two of you and Sam and Ben to be available as well. In the meantime, get Chuck to run a test on the phone system, just to be sure we're clean."

"You really think the phones are tapped, Jake?" asked Tina, still in shock over what she just heard. "How's that possible? We certainly would've picked up on that by now."

"We didn't have reason to believe so, but be sure Chuck runs the test."

"OK," answered Tina as she stood to leave. "Anything else? Oh, be sure and check out your other messages. There's one from Grace."

"Will do, thanks. OK, that's all for now."

He sat back down and dialed the 4-Poster and asked Marge if Grace was still around. She put her hand over the receiver and whispered to Lucy, "Go tell Grace she has a call. Tell her it's from Sheriff Jake. Hurry, hurry."

"So, how are things at the department?" she began when she saw Grace coming in from the porch. Before he could answer, Marge said, "Oh, never mind. We can catch up later, here's Grace."

"Good morning, Jake," Grace said. "It's good to hear your voice. I had such a wonderful time yesterday. I'd really like to see you. Any chance we could meet for lunch at the diner around noonish?"

"Possibly. But, I can't take much time. Something's come up here and I have to be back by 2:00."

There was a long pause.

"Grace. You still there?"

"Well, Jake. If you can't make it. It's OK," she said. Maybe he's trying to pull back, she thought.

"No, no, noon will be fine. I'll meet you there, OK?"

"Good. Bye for now."

And now for my famous juggling act Jake thought. What a week. And it's just beginning.

Twenty-five

Jake left his desk and went into the squad room. Most of the men were there this morning. Chuck was standing beside Turner's desk with a disassembled phone in his hand. Jake motioned him to come over to him.

"So, how's it going so far?"

"Nothing so far to report. I just don't see how a wiretap could be put on our phones without our knowing it. I'm almost done with the phones themselves. Do you know when the tap was supposed to have been put in place?"

"No, sorry."

"Well this is how it works, Jake," Chuck said. "You know all of our phones are hooked up to the same system and calls are recorded, incoming and outgoing. A wiretap would just show up as an additional extension. We normally have no need to listen to the tapes and only keep them for a month at

96

a time. Then they're erased. Now, Jake, the hard part, or should I say the boring part. I'm going to have to sit and listen to all of them and see if I can determine if that additional extension exists and who tapped in on us. It'll take some time. I apologize in advance to anyone who had a personal conversation not meant for me to hear, but, well, they knew about the tape recorder capturing the conversations. On the other hand, it may be pretty interesting. I understand blackmail pays pretty well?" Chuck smiled.

"Get out of here, Chuck, and get going before you say anything else you'll regret later. And keep in mind, this really isn't a joking situation."

"Sorry, Chief."

"That's OK. Now see if you can have the report back to me before 3:00."

Jake thought the mayor should be apprised of the situation, but that would have to wait until the Feds' arrival and their meeting. He pulled out a list of deputies he had available and wondered now if he had enough ready to be called in for active duty if the town's threat level suddenly changed. He was already stretched with Summerfair security. He'd wait before handing out any new assignments. He pulled out the list of available deputies based in Farmsville. If things go bad, they'd also be needed. Sheriff Grady was always accommodating when he needed extra help. That would give him about forty-five to pull from. That made him feel more comfortable.

He looked at his watch. 11:00. He looked down at the remaining messages that had come in before he arrived. One of the messages was from the Fulmer man who wanted to know if they had found out anything about the lights yet. Great, Jake thought, the lights. Strangely, no one's mentioned seeing them for some time. He hadn't given up on that mystery yet.

The second message, wasn't really a message. Tina just noted that after she identified herself, a man asked to speak to Sheriff Mason then hung up, leaving no message. The reason she left the note for him was that the caller sounded a lot like the man in the Mets cap at the diner.

Jake kept both of the messages where he could find them again.

On his way out, Jake stopped at Clyde's desk.

"Be sure Ben and Sam are here when the Feds arrive at 3:00. Let's be sure we're all here by 2 actually. I want to use my office. I don't know how many agents will be coming with Special Agent Quinn. Hopefully we'll have enough seats. Bring in a couple of extra folding chairs just in case if you would. Thanks. Gotta go."

As Jake turned to leave, Clyde called after him. "Enjoy your lunch, Casanova."

Jake just shook his head. He could see Clyde wasn't letting go of this one.

Twenty-six

When Jake arrived at the diner, he looked around the line of people in front of him waiting for tables. He spotted Grace sitting in a booth in back. Above her a picture of Mayor Wilkes, wearing his signature red polka dot bow tie, smiled down upon her.

Below the mayor's frozen grin, Grace by contrast looked distracted. Jake noticed she was unconsciously twisting her mother's bracelet round and round on her wrist. He watched her for a few moments. She finally looked in his direction. Her face relaxed. She smiled at him with that inviting smile of hers. That smile always pulled him to her physically and emotionally.

"Well, it makes me happy to see you again, Grace," Jake said as he slid into the seat across from her.

"You've brightened up my day too, Jake."

He reached over and took her hands in his.

"Let's just acknowledge we had a great time together and let things happen as they happen. Look, I've got to be back at the office at 2:00, but, how about this. It's such a beautiful day. Let's grab a couple of sandwiches and head out to my beach house. It's so pretty out there and the two of us can have an oceanside picnic. What do you say?"

Just then, Dolores appeared at their table to take their order.

"Hi, Dolores. I was just trying to convince Grace here, that it's too nice to stay inside. We need to have a picnic."

He looked over at Grace. "How about it, game?"

"Sounds great!" Grace answered enthusiastically. "Let's see. How about a tuna salad sandwich, Dolores?"

"Make it two," Jake added. "We'll meet you at the counter and let some of these tourists have our booth."

Jake put in a call to the station and asked Turner if he'd bring the cruiser down to the diner. That way they could save time. Twenty minutes later, Jake and Grace were on the beach road headed for Jake's house.

He rolled down both windows as far as they'd go. The blue sky was cloudless. The onshore breeze created small breakers on the ocean, sending the warm moist scent of the sea shoreward. He looked over at Grace, whose face was turned toward the ocean enjoying every moment of the experience.

"What a wonderful idea, Jake," she said, "just wonderful."

As they pulled into the driveway of the white-washed cottage, he noticed the neighbor's dog, Rex, in the next yard sleeping under one of the scrub bushes. He hadn't seen him for a while.

"Before we go in, I wanted to tell you, the interior isn't all my doing. My Dad did most of the decorating early on. I think I told you he'd owned his own charter fishing business. Just wanted you to know that's why there's a stuffed fish mounted over the sink in the kitchen."

Grace loved to hear Jake ramble on, so she just smiled and hung on his words.

"We had some good times together. He was a great dad. When he came here to Maine, he brought a lot of Mom's favorite things. He couldn't bear to think of life without her. I think he tried to arrange everything the way he thought Mom would like it, notwithstanding the mounted trout in the kitchen. You'll see tons of family pictures and I haven't had time to hide my goofy childhood photos. Try not to embarrass me by laughing. Promise?"

"We'll see," she responded with a grin. "No promises."

Grace looked around the living room as she entered. Straight ahead of her, floor to ceiling windows faced out onto a wide flagstone patio that looked across an expanse of endless ocean. From there, fifty feet of white sand led to the water's edge. Turning her head to the right, she saw the kitchen through an open doorway. There was a hallway to her left, which she surmised led to the bedroom area. As he promised, the room was filled with photos and memorabilia.

"Jake, this is so charming, so warm and inviting. I love it. Now where did you say those baby pictures are hiding?"

She looked over at Jake. He was staring at a photo of his dad on the mantle of the fireplace. He looked so serious all of a sudden. She recalled how emotional he had grown during their dinner at the fair when he talked about his father.

"You OK, Jake?"

"Yeah. Let's sit for a minute. I just remembered

this was the day Dad died four years ago."

"Oh, I'm so sorry, Jake," she said following him into the living room.

"It's OK. I try not to think about it, but when the day rolls around again, I can't help it."

She felt Jake's sadness. She never knew her father. "Oh Jake. It's OK to be sad. You were blessed to have someone in your life like that. It'll get easier as the years pass. He'll always be close to you."

"I'm sorry, Grace. We came here to have a good time; I didn't intend to..."

"No, no, come on. It's all right."

"Yeah, he was quite a guy. He enjoyed life."

"Well Jake, he'd want nothing less than for you to do the same, don't you think?"

"You're right, you're right, Grace. Thanks for listening. I'm OK now."

He took a deep breath. "Look, I'll get us some cold drinks from the kitchen. Why don't you go out and see if you can put up the beach umbrella on the table? I'll bring the sandwiches. I think I have some chips too. Be right there."

When Grace opened the patio doors, the sea breeze filled the room.

"You should leave these doors open all the time you're home. Isn't the breeze wonderful." She inhaled deeply, filling her lungs with the fresh ocean air. I could settle down here, she thought. What a daydream...but such a good one.

Her mind momentarily went back to Vorack, what she had to do in the next few days and what lay ahead of her. No, she said to herself, and forced the thoughts to stop.

Until she met Jake, she never wanted to change the life she'd been leading for so many years. She never thought it possible to go in any other direction. But suddenly, her life was filling with new meaning. Much to her surprise, in the short time she'd known him, she found herself falling in love. She embraced this moment she was sharing with him. She felt she'd earned it.

When lunch was over, Jake looked at his watch. 1:15. Grace now leaned against the kitchen door frame watching him put everything away. Starting to reach into the refrigerator for another couple of cold drinks to take with them, he glanced over at her. There she was looking so desirable. He stopped what he was doing when their eyes met.

"You do nice work," she teased.

He smiled back at her. "Oh, I'm very good at what I do."

As if time stood still, they remained silently staring at one another. Her eyes said it all. Jake walked over to her and drew her close to him in a welcomed embrace.

She held him tightly and wouldn't let go.

Jake looked down into those sensuous green eyes staring up at him. "I want you so much, Grace."

He tilted her face toward his and kissed her deeply. The heat from his desire for her filled her with excitement.

Twenty-seven

When Grace arrived back at the 4-Poster after being with Jake at the beach house, she hardly noticed the parlor filled with chatting people in the middle of afternoon tea, or a woman carrying a small sleeping child headed down the hall on the way to their room. As she put her key into the lock, she inhaled the aroma of the pink rose in its tiny vase on her front door. It all seemed as if she were still the leading lady in a wonderful, exciting dream.

She laid down on her back on the bed and stared up at the white ceiling above her. It was a movie screen to her on which she could reenact the wonderful, emotional scenes she'd played in that afternoon. She didn't want the movie to end.

She sighed, and finally made herself get up. She crossed the room and pulled out her backpack. She started to fill it once more, being sure to stuff the small toy dog Jake had won for her down in the bottom of the bag. She liked to think of mini-Maxie as her watchdog. After changing into her hiking clothes, she scanned the room.

Closing the door, this time, she hung her key and the sealed note to Jake on a hook below the bud vase. She shut her eyes and inhaled the sweet aroma of the tiny rose once again. She wanted to tuck that memory away for later. She couldn't bear to tell Jake she was leaving when they parted. She hoped the note would keep him from being concerned, or worse, suspicious of her behavior.

The last thing she did before locking the door was to pick up her phone. She punched in the same sequence of numbers and waited for a reply. Upon hearing the voice at the other end, she spoke four words into the receiver, "Mother, I have arrived." There was a pause, then she ended the short conversation by saying, "I'm on my way," and hung up.

Two hours later, Grace arrived at Morefield House. Dimitri greeted her, as he had the first time she arrived there.

"We missed you, Grace," Dimitri said as he opened the back door for her.

"I'll bet," she responded.

When she came to the bottom of the stairs, everyone turned around. Natasia greeted her saying she was happy to have another woman to talk to for a change. Grace went into the sleeping quarters, threw her backpack onto her bed, and went back and joined the others.

"See," began Sergei, "We have all the equipment you asked for. See over there," he said pointing to the side of the wall facing away from the group. "We put you there so you'd have a place of your own to spread out and not have to listen to Natasia's chatter."

Natasia gave Sergei a punch in his left shoulder. "Ouch. You've got to watch out for her. She's a dangerous woman."

Maxim was busy showing Dimitri some new intel coming in. Grace overheard him ask Dimitri if he should wait to see how it would play out or contact the Major now. Dimitri advised him to give it until morning. There could be more detailed info by then.

Grace sat down at the computer and started typing. A series of numbers and symbols cascaded down the screen. The scrolling stopped and a picture of the front of the Caswell Bay Sheriff's Department filled the screen. She picked up the headphones and listened. Nothing.

"Dimitri," she began. "I'm not getting any feedback from the wiretap at the station. Why not?"

"Here, let me try. Give me the headphones." He started typing. The screen flickered, losing the picture of the department for a moment. Then it appeared once more.

"Damn," he muttered. "They must have found the tap and disabled it. That could only mean one thing. The Feds are here now." He glanced up at the screen. "Look, look there, in front of the station, that van. It has to be Feds. Rerun the tape from the light pole feed. Take it back slowly."

Grace started the rerun.

"Stop there. Look, look at the four men and a woman getting out of the van. They're talking to your boyfriend, the sheriff."

Grace blushed and hoped no one noticed.

"They've got to be Feds," Dimitri said. "The intel was right. We need to get ahold of the Major with this one. I told him he should have one of his precious spybirds sitting up there instead of the piece of crap he had me install. If he'd done that, we could have heard what they were saying. 'No, no,' he said. 'The wiretap will tell us what we want to know.' Well, let's see how he feels now. Of course, he'll never admit having made a mistake, the old bastard."

The others were gathered around now watching the video.

"Maxim, you have other cameras up. Didn't Karl install them somewhere else in town?"

"Sure, sure."

"See if this van shows up in any of the others. Do it now," Dimitri barked orders to him like a drill sergeant. "We need to see where they've set up their surveillance center. Oh, I wish I knew what was said inside that building."

"Hey, Grace. I bet you can get old Jake to give you some info if you handle it just right. When are you going to see him again?"

"Well, not until I leave this grand hotel, that's for sure. And just how should I go about getting the info out of him?"

"You're a Russian agent, come on, like you've never done that before. So make him like you, screw him."

"OK," said Sergei. "That's enough. You kiddies play nice now before Uncle Sergei has to put you in your room."

Grace and Dimitri glared at one another.

Dimitri's angry glare turned toward Sergei. "Get me Vorack. Now."

"Wait, Dimitri," said Maxim, turning away from his screen. "I found the van again. It's headed north out of town. Don't know where it ended up."

"OK, well, at least we have a direction. I imagine

the Major will send one of us that way to see if we can find their secret hideout."

Sergei motioned Dimitri to come over and sit at his table. The Major was waiting to talk to him.

"Hello, Major," Dimitri began and then reiterated the story that just unfolded. No one could hear the Major's responses, but could tell by Dimitri's side of the conversation he certainly wasn't happy about anything Dimitri was telling him.

When the conversation ended, everyone stood like bowling pins in an alley waiting for a strike to wipe them out. Nothing the Major did was ever welcome.

"Well—well what did he say?" Sergei asked fearfully.

"You won't believe it," Dimitri said. "He actually said he wished he'd used one of his spybirds to capture the info. I couldn't believe it. He said he was going to send Karl out before daylight tomorrow to find the Fed's secret location. Karl will have a spybird with him to install—in invisible mode of course—to monitor their activities."

Dimitri paused, then turned to Grace. "He had a message for you Grace. He wants you to hurry up and hack into the Fed's communication lines. Between you, the FBI mole, and the spybird, it should give him the heads up on their movements and plans, giving him time to complete the mission. And work on the sheriff to get as much info from him as you can. Whatever you find out, the Major must know immediately."

Sergei opened his mouth, ready to speak, but Dimitri shushed him with a glare. "Time's running short, very short," he snapped. "I have it from a good source that the Major intends to wrap this mission up by next weekend. He wants to leave Fisher Island while Summerfair is on and the security forces will be preoccupied. I don't know if he'll be coming back or what'll happen to the base, or to us, as a matter of fact. Hopefully, that means we'll finally be getting out of this place too. No celebration yet. Grace, get to work. That goes for the rest of you too."

Late that afternoon, Grace felt her cell phone vibrating in her pocket. "I need a break," she told Natasia.

Natasia looked over at Dimitri, who nodded his approval. After Grace exited through the kitchen door, she moved to the front of the house out of earshot of anyone inside. She pulled out her phone and checked the number of the incoming call.

She dialed and waited. She listened carefully to the voice at the other end of the line and answered in response to the questions: "Yes, that's OK. No, not yet; I want to take care of that myself. Soon. Yes, I heard you," she said adamantly. "I'll be ready."

She placed the phone into her pants pocket and returned to the basement.

Grace wondered, if Vorack could get that kind of information, why did he really need her to hack their system? Even though it didn't seem so, there must be a limited amount this mole is privy to. At least for the moment, Vorack didn't know about her—yet.

Twenty-eight

Jake parked his cruiser and saw Turner at the head of the stairs.

"Everyone here?" Jake asked him as he hurried by him and in through the front door.

"Yes, Chief."

"Thanks. Talk to you inside."

Clyde stood talking to Sam, both men parked in Tina's doorway. As Clyde turned around, Jake could see something was wrong by the look on his face.

"Jake, Chuck found evidence someone's been listening in on our conversations for the last month at least," Clyde said. "He couldn't find the source. There was no listing for the number of the incoming calls. He was able to disable the system and remove the added extension, so we're OK for now. We still don't know how they managed to do it. Anyway, it's taken care of."

"That's a shocker. I need Chuck's report asap."

"It's already on your desk, Chief."

Jake motioned to Clyde to follow him into his office. He did a quick visual scan of his now cleaned up desktop. Tina must have come in while he was gone. Jake smiled and shook his head. He saw Chuck's report sitting on top of his wire basket. He looked quickly around the room and back at Clyde.

"Tina got a call from your Agent Quinn a half hour ago," Clyde said. "She said there'd be five of them today. They should be here any time now. Quinn said she's going to take the meeting without her agents being present."

"OK. That'll work. Ask Tina to have some coffee brewing. We can always send out for something to eat depending on how late the meeting runs. I'd like Tina in here to take notes during the meeting. Well, actually, I'd really like to record the meeting. Get the small tape recorder and we'll use that one. Let Turner handle incoming calls when we start our talk. Tell him whoever they want to talk to is in a meeting and we'll call them back. If it's an emergency, I'd like to know right away."

Jake looked up at the clock. "Almost time, Clyde. I need a moment or two. I'm going to wait outside and see what they roll up in."

Opening the front door, Jake carried a cup of coffee with him and leaned on the railing just outside the front door of the department. He kept thinking about Grace and their afternoon together. He was looking forward to meeting her at the 4-Poster later.

He wished he had a cigarette, but he'd stopped smoking months ago. Just as he looked down to check his watch, a black Mercedes van pulled up to

111

the curb. The four van doors opened at the same time. A woman stepped out of the front passenger side. Three men joining her waited for the driver to come around the front of the van. Then the five of them started up the steps.

The woman looked up at Jake, who hadn't moved from where he was standing.

"I'm looking for Sheriff Mason."

"I'm Sheriff Mason," Jake said extending his hand to her. "You must be Special Agent Quinn. Welcome."

As they entered the building Jake said, "I'd like you to meet my Chief Deputy, Clyde Thompson and my dispatcher, Tina Davis. You'll be working closely with the two of them."

He motioned to the other men to join them. "Over here are two of my deputies, Chuck Jackson and Ben Clemans. Standing behind Deputy Clemans is Sergeant Sam Owens. Deputy Turner seems to be missing at the moment."

Just at that moment, Turner came back into the room. "And Special Agent Quinn, this is our newest officer, Deputy Turner Ward." Turner nodded and looked a little embarrassed not to have been present when they arrived.

"Good to meet you all," Quinn replied. "I'd like you to meet my agents, George Jenkins, Mike Flynn, Javier Cortes and Bob Knox." All nodded in response. "They're a special unit trained in counter terrorism. We also have a helicopter at our disposal five miles north of here. We can have others here too if needed."

"Well, Agent Quinn, this really does sound serious," Jake said. "How about coming into my office and finding a chair. Coffee's on the table over there. Help yourself. Clyde, Tina, join us."

Tina, the last to enter, closed the door and closed the blinds separating the office from the squad room.

After all were seated, Jake looked over at Agent Quinn. "Just to let you know, we did find a wiretap on our phones. There was no way to determine who was listening. The phone number went nowhere. Thanks for the heads up."

Agent Quinn nodded.

"Now let's hear your story," Jake said.

"We're trying to apprehend a known terrorist who's been traced to your city," Quinn began. "We're staying in mobile housing units brought in by the Bureau just outside of town near an abandoned quarry. One will be used as our communication center. We want to keep as secretive as possible."

Jake looked over at Tina and nodded. She reached forward and turned on the tape recorder.

Quinn held up her hand. "Wait, Sheriff, you can't record this meeting,"

"I want to review our conversation later, to be sure we have all the correct information," Jake explained. "It's important I make appropriate decisions in this case."

"Look, Sheriff Mason, this is our case. We'll be calling the shots."

"I don't think so, Agent Quinn. Not as long as you're in my jurisdiction. We will work as a team."

"That's not the way we operate, Sheriff."

"And I'm not trying to tell you how to do your job, Agent Quinn. We're ready to cooperate fully with the FBI in finding this perpetrator," Jake said.

"But we go into this as equal partners."

Agent Quinn wasn't happy, but she grudgingly agreed. He's living up to his reputation, she thought, having read his dossier. "Stop there for a moment, sheriff. I need to put in a call to the Director. Excuse the interruption. I'll be right back."

Clyde looked over at Jake.

A few moments later, Agent Quinn opened the door. "Sorry about that, Sheriff Mason. I needed to confer with the Director. You and your chief deputy here will be updated with all the information we've gathered to date. If you trust your dispatcher I'll include her as well. Full secrecy is expected. No information leaves this room."

"I told the Director, I felt that you are to be trusted and you and your staff would be invaluable in the capture of this man. After our discussion, he gave me permission to bring you in fully."

"Amen. Now the sparing match is over," Jake said.

"Answer this first, Sheriff. When did you say this Summerfair opens?"

"The artists and merchants will start setting up in less than a week. They open for business on Saturday morning at 9 just before the parade. The show runs until 8 in the evening. It opens again on Sunday morning at 10 and closes at five."

"Not much time, but doable," Agent Quinn commented. "We're concerned the large influx of people could give this man and his cohorts a better chance to disappear. Our hope is to grab him before the weekend."

"We've been looking for a Russian Agent, a Major Anton Vorack," Quinn said. "And we know where he's located, at least for the present. We've found evidence that he was involved in the bombing of our US embassy in Tehran in 1980. The US Ambassador, Alexander Freeman, was seriously wounded and four members of his staff were killed. Vorack was also rumored to have an important role in the bombing of Holt Federal Building in Dallas five years later. We lost thirty-four people."

Quinn paused, as she and all in the room pondered the loss of American lives Vorack left in his wake.

"The Major surfaced in Paris two years later and then went underground again," Quinn continued. "With the help from a Russian snitch, the agency learned that he was in Boston, Massachusetts in November of 1991. There was a possible sighting in Portland, Maine in 1994. We've now narrowed the trail to a twenty-mile area of possibility. Someone we'd been tracking who'd worked with him in Boston, a Dimitri Povash, was reportedly seen here in your town about a week ago."

Agent Quinn opened her valise and removed a large folder. She slid several photos across the table to Jake.

"Have you seen this man here in Caswell Bay?"

The first photo showed a young man in army fatigues with a rifle over one shoulder. Only his profile was visible in the picture as he stood facing another soldier in some outdoor encampment. The second photo was clearer and showed a young soldier walking alone beside a piece of artillery equipment. In the third photo, he was in civilian clothes, casually dressed, standing on a street corner looking up toward a traffic light waiting for it to change.

"Do you have a close-up of this one?" Jake asked, pointing to the third photo.

"Yes."

The minute Jake saw it, it reminded him of the hooded male figure he saw in the diner about a week ago.

"Yes, I may have seen him at our local diner about seven days ago. Tina, come over here and look at this photo. Could this be the man in the Mets cap you saw there a couple of days later?"

"That's him, Sheriff."

"Good." Agent Quinn continued, "He's an assassin for hire wanted on three continents. He's responsible for multiple deaths. We know he has a role in Major Vorack's plans. I'd like you to ask your men to be on the lookout for this man Povash. Tell us who he associates with. We can't let the Major escape this time."

"Fulmer," Jake blurted out. He looked over at Clyde. "Remember Larry Fulmer, the man who saw a person fitting Povash's description headed up to Hawksview Ridge? It was right after the sighting of the weird lights."

He looked back at Agent Quinn. "Every once in a while there's a reporting of what looks like a signal from Fisher Island. Lights flash on and off. We've been out there three or four times but we haven't found anything suspicious. There must be a connection between Povash, the lights, and probably the Major. Go on, Agent Quinn."

"Sheriff, that jibes with what we've discovered," Quinn said. "Vorack has set up a three-story laboratory system underneath Fisher Island. They're using the Morefield House as a communication center. They communicate using flashing lights between the mainland and the island."

Jake was stunned. How could this supposed laboratory be built under his very nose?

"What do you mean inside Fisher Island? How inside?"

"Well, we don't know how he was able to hollow out the island without its collapse, but he did and has a base there with scientists and agents. It took a long time. It was a slow process. We can show you how we think it happened, but it's not important right now. The important objective is to stop the Major."

"And how did you learn all of this?"

"We have a source."

"What's that supposed to mean? What source?"

"Well, that's all I can tell you right now."

Jake stood up again, facing Agent Quinn.

"What do you mean that's all you can tell me? There's a terrorist in my town and you just now inform me? What kind of agency are you?"

"Look, Sheriff, we're still missing the information about his plan and how he intends to execute it," Quinn said. "What if we had given your office the word and it leaked. Or worse, somehow or other the island was raided prematurely and Vorack warned. We just couldn't risk it until all the elements were in play."

Jake moved back behind his desk and sat down. The room was deadly silent. Jake looked over at Agent Quinn across from him.

"We're certain something big is set for this weekend during Summerfair," she said. "We have to get this man. Can you get over yourself and continue to give us your ideas and assistance in capturing this terrorist?"

"Of course," Jake shot back. "You don't have to ask me that question. This operation isn't about me. This terrorist's got to be stopped. But you listen to me, Special Agent Quinn. There's nothing more important to me than the safety of this town and its inhabitants. Agreed?"

"I understand, Sheriff. I'll be as cooperative as possible."

"Agent Quinn, I'd like us to form a team of my men and your agents and go up to the Morefield House tomorrow," Jake said. "Who we find there, if anyone, could solve this whole mystery. We'll be prepared for confrontation, just in case. Maybe we'll get lucky."

"Agreed. A raid is warranted. You know the area. What's the plan?"

"I'd like to start in the morning as soon as it's daylight," Jake said. "It's a long trip up, about three hours. It's impossible to make that trip to the Ridge using the forest trail. We'll have to skirt around town and go up through the old service road that used to go to Farmsville. It runs right behind the Morefield House. It's clear most of the way, but I think we'd better take the bulldozer. We can take heavier vehicles as well. I don't know if anyone occupying the house would even know about the road. All those tall bushes near the house make the road impossible to see. The undergrowth will give us some cover as well."

"Sheriff, I want to call the Director and tell him the plan," Quinn said. "You've been a great help. I know he'll be pleased with his decision to bring you in. I can see we'll get a lot accomplished working as a team. In the meantime, I need to get back with the others. How about, we be here tomorrow morning, say, 6 a.m.?"

"Fine. You know how to reach us if you need to. We'll see you in the morning."

"Oh, and sheriff, be sure you lock up those tapes."

Jake smiled. She doesn't leave any loose ends.

After Quinn and her agents left, Jake asked Tina to make some copies of the Povash picture and told Clyde to be sure all the officers had one. They weren't to post or pass out the photo, just watch for the man.

After the FBI left, Jake asked Tina to have Ben, Sam, and Chuck come into his office. He needed to get everyone prepared for the morning. He thought he'd tell them the FBI was here looking for someone and thought they could be holed up in the Morefield House. That should do for the moment.

On the way back to their temporary base of operations, Agent Quinn asked Cortes to pull over. She needed to make a phone call. She stepped out of earshot and faced away from the car. Placing the call, she waited, but there wasn't an answer. She'd wait a few moments longer and see if there'd be a response. There was. After delivering her message, she wasn't entirely happy with the answer she'd received.

Twenty-nine

While Jake waited for the others to come in, he looked over at Clyde.

"Well now, wasn't that a revelation? And we were worried about Summerfair."

"Jake. This is big! Have you ever run into a situation like this before?" asked Clyde.

"Well Clyde, back in Los Angeles, we dealt with a lot of shady characters, dangerous men, heads of syndicates. I think, with the FBI and a beefed up task force here, we have a good chance of catching this guy. I want the patrols to double up, more men, more often, more eyes everywhere. As Agent Quinn said, if we can spot this Povash once, especially since he doesn't know we're onto him, we may be able to spot him again."

Jake rose from his chair and pulled down a city map on the far wall. "The FBI will have their men infiltrating the town right away. We need to be able to identify them too. I'll talk to Quinn about that. It's so crowded in town now that the perps have a lot of cover. We don't know how many people are working with this Major."

Jake gestured toward the map. "You can see there are endless places to blend in right now."

Jake took out a box of tiny red flags and began sticking them into strategic places on the map.

"Clyde, I'd like you to place our men in these locations but on a rotating schedule. I only want half of them in uniform. A security presence is expected, but not plainclothesmen. I'll call Sheriff Grady over in Farmsville and ask him if he could spare ten of his men to help us out at Summerfair this coming week. They won't be recognizable by the locals. Agent Quinn and I will go over the roster and ID the men and women being used."

By 5 p.m. Jake had laid out plans for the next day with Sam and Ben and closed the door to his office. He picked up the phone and dialed the 4-Poster.

"4-Poster, Marge speaking."

"Hello, Marge. This is Jake. Can you locate Grace for me? I'd like to talk to her."

"Hold the phone, Jake. I'll look, but I haven't seen her around. I'll go upstairs and check her room as well. Be right back."

Jake waited, sitting tapping his pencil on the desktop. She's taking too long he thought. Something's not right. His heart sank when he heard Marge's voice back on the phone.

"She's not here, Jake. There's an envelope hanging on the door with your name on it. I can open it and read it to you if you like."

Jake pressed the pencil into the table top, breaking off the lead point.

"No thanks, Marge. I think I'll drop by and pick

it up."

"OK, see you soon," she replied and hung up.

Jake thought, not again. What could possibly have gone wrong after their being together earlier. Was she having second thoughts? She hadn't mentioned having to go away. She had to have known. He checked around his office and waved goodbye.

"See you in the morning, Jake," Tina called back.

He walked over to Clyde. "Someday, huh, Clyde? Try and get some rest. Be sure the men have protective gear and we have enough ammo."

As Clyde took notes, Jake continued.

"Call Agent Quinn and tell her when we're all together in the morning, I want to go over the attack plans again and make sure everyone knows what they're supposed to do. OK, well I guess that's all for now. I've got to go over to the 4-Poster. See you in the morning."

Clyde gave Jake a knowing smile. "The 4-Poster? Right. OK, I'll talk to Quinn. See ya in the morning, Chief."

Jake took the cruiser. It didn't take long to get to the 4-Poster. Marge handed him the sealed envelope, then left.

"My girls and I are in the back garden if you need anything, Jake," she said as she left. He sat in one of the swings on the front porch with the sealed envelope in his hand, not wanting to open it.

Jake could hear Marge's nieces singing a song Jake almost remembered from his childhood, their voices wafting from the back garden. Marge must have taught it to them. He ran his finger under the sealed flap and opened the envelope. He recognized

Grace's neat handwriting and read the note.

I'm sorry to do this to you again, Jake, but something's happened. I have to leave for a few days. You know how it is when a lead comes up. You just have to follow it before it disappears. The timing is especially bad after today. I can't tell you how much I'd rather be with you. Keep the memory of our afternoon in your mind. I promise, when I come back, we'll create even better ones.
Love, Grace.

Jake was annoyed. He folded up the letter and stuck it in his breast pocket. What's wrong with this picture, he thought to himself. What is wrong? She had to have known she was leaving again. What's she hiding from him? Is she even writing a story? He's never seen any evidence of one and she never says much about what she does while she's away. As he recalled, she changed the subject when he pressed her for more details.

And what was she doing going out to Fisher Island the day they met? Now that he knew what was going on out there, he wondered if the reason for her trip was the truth. Is she really who she claims to be? That's it. Before going home, he'd stop at the department. If Clyde's still there, he'd have him run a background check on her.

Suddenly, Jake got up and peered through the screen door. Seeing no one in sight, he opened it quietly and headed for the stairs to the second floor. He remembered Grace had mentioned she was staying in Room 4. When he reached the door, he removed the key from its hook and went in, closing the door silently behind him.

Just as Grace had last scanned the room before she left three hours earlier, Jake let his eyes review its contents. But Jake was viewing it now as a detective entering a crime scene. He wanted to be thorough. He hoped to find something that would help him explain her behavior.

He reminded himself, it could just be her zeal at wanting to be a good investigative reporter. He wanted to believe that was the case. At that moment, he started to feel he'd made the wrong move coming up to her room. Jake felt like a heel for not trusting the woman he had come to love. But something compelled him to continue his search.

He slipped on a pair of latex gloves and went over to the wardrobe. Nothing but clothes hung neatly inside. He pulled one of Grace's dresses toward him and inhaled her scent, then replaced it carefully just as he'd found it. He closed the wardrobe and quietly opened each dresser drawer. Again, nothing unusual.

He ran his hands down the bed linens and under the comforter and raised up the mattress and looked under it and under the bed itself. His eyes caught sight of a dark green suitcase. Pulling it out, he flipped open the latches. Empty. He pushed it back underneath.

As he sat down on the bed, he noticed a pad and pencil on the nightstand. Something she'd written on the pad had left a deep impression. He picked up the notepad and the pencil next to it and walked over to the window. Taking the pencil and carefully turning the lead tip on its side, he ran it softly back and forth across the indentation. The pencil slipped out of his hand and fell to the floor. A single word became visible. "Vorack!"

Shocked by the discovery, Jake just stood there for a moment. He tore off the sheet of paper and carefully folded it and put it in his pocket. He replaced the pad and pencil back on the nightstand. He returned the ornate key to the hook on her front door and quickly moved down the empty staircase, leaving the 4-Poster undiscovered.

Before Jake started the motor, he sat in his cruiser for some time trying to put the puzzle together.

Grace, he thought, oh, Grace. Who are you?

Thirty

On his way back to the beach house, Jake stopped at the department. He was in luck. He saw Clyde's van still parked in front. Clyde had just finished up a report and was getting ready to lock up, when he heard Jake come through the door.

"Clyde, old buddy. You're still here."

"I know that tone of voice. What do you want me to do?"

"I know it's late. But before you go, do me a favor. I know it's an odd request, but I'd like you to run a background check on Grace Cooper. I need it asap. In fact, is it possible to get it now?"

"On Grace?" Clyde asked with dismay. But one look at Jake's face stilled any further questions. "Yes, it's possible. It'll take about an hour. I'll do it for you. Let me call Esther and let her know I'll be late."

Jake left and made a short stop at the Food Mart

on his way home. By the time he turned the key in the lock of the beach house, the phone was ringing.

He tossed the food bag on a chair and grabbed the phone.

"So Clyde, tell me about our investigative reporter. What did you find out?"

"Not a great deal, Jake. But everything she told you checked out. I've got a copy of her birth certificate and social security info in front of me. It says here that she was born in Holworth, Nebraska in 1965, but doesn't say anything about her parents or if she has any siblings. She went to Longbrook College in Omaha and graduated in 1988. I saw a copy of her transcript from Boston College, where she later took a course in investigative journalism. There's a sample pay stub for her library work. She worked there for three years. It doesn't say why she went to Boston, only that she lived there for four years. I didn't find a record of her current address there, if she still has one. That's about all there is. It's not as complete as I'd have expected, but again, does match what she's told us."

"Thanks a lot, Clyde, appreciate it."

"Jake, if you don't mind my asking, why the background check?"

Jake had never lied to Clyde before. But he just had to confront Grace first.

"It's big," Jake said. "That's all I can say right now. Talk to you later."

And it was over. No new clues at all. Jake thought he'd just have to wait, but not for long.

He fixed himself a Manhattan and went outside to his patio. He pulled up a deck chair and sat watching the clouds in the sky turn from orange to grey, the blackness of night ready to settle in around him. Soon, the last of his Manhattan rested on a table next to his lounge chair. The breeze was cooling and he started to feel just relaxed enough to close his eyes.

He kept seeing the notepad paper in front of him bearing the name, "Vorack!" He wondered where Grace really was at the moment. Keeping this information from the FBI or even Clyde could and should wreck his career. But, he wanted to confront Grace himself—and—alone. But that too could be risky. If, indeed, she was a Russian spy, she could see him now as expendable. Was she just using him to get information? But to what end?

Knowing that there was a connection between the lights, the Morefield House and the island, explained a lot of things. And he'd found Grace headed out to it in a boat. Why?

Enough for tonight, he thought. A blanket of stars now covered the moonlit sky. It had to be late. He checked his watch, 11:00. He locked up and laid down on his bed and tried to sleep. Perhaps tomorrow, Morefield House would reveal more than he'd expected.

Thirty-one

Grace lay on her bed in the basement of the Morefield House, thinking of Jake and how often these sudden departures from his life had become. Be real, she told herself. As much as she'd come to care for Jake, they had no future together. She'd either have to tell him the truth and suffer the consequences of deceiving him, or leave when the mission was over and never look back.

The phone, now hidden under her pillow, began to vibrate. It startled Grace. She looked around the room at the sleeping agents. She turned over and sat up. There wasn't any place for her to go except outside. She hoped no one would wake up and go searching for her. She stuck her pillows under her covers to make it appear that she was still there.

The sleeping quarters were almost pitch black as she moved toward the next room. Maxim mumbled something in his sleep. She stopped. Grace held her

129

breath, then she heard his snoring resume. She continued up the stairs and sat outside the back door. The full moon cast deep, ominous shadows across the yard, making Grace anxious to get back inside.

She picked up the phone and redialed the recent incoming number. She knew who it was and knew the message was important.

When the connection was made, Grace asked in a voice just above a whisper, "Why are you calling me again? What's the matter?"

"You've got to get out of there before 0900."

"What?" Grace responded in total shock. "Why?"

"Raid! Move out without creating any suspicion."

The line went dead.

Grace returned inside and slipped back under the covers just as Dimitri sat up. Leaning on one elbow, he looked up at her.

"Grace," he whispered. "Where've you been?"

"Bathroom," Grace replied without hesitation.

"Oh, OK."

Grace sighed deeply, thinking about escape and what the raid meant for the mission. How would Vorack respond to the discovery and capture of his men. Would that stop his mission?

At 6:00, Sergei got up and made a pot of coffee. Still half asleep, coffee in hand, he walked across the room and turned on the light over his workbench, accidentally moving the computer mouse on top of the table. The screen on his computer came to life; large blinking letters spelled out "Urgent!" "Urgent!" "Urgent!"

Now wide awake, he typed in the password used to receive encrypted messages from the Major.

Hopefully this one would come in intact. It did. It took him an endless ten minutes to decipher it.

The message read: ABANDON THE HOUSE IMMEDIATELY. THE FBI AND THE SHERIFF AND HIS MEN ARE COMING TO THE HOUSE THIS MORNING. THEY WILL BE THERE BEFORE 10:00.

SAVE ALL THE INFORMATION YOU HAVE ON DISCS AND WIPE THE COMPUTERS CLEAN. DESTROY THE COMPUTERS AND ANY EVIDENCE THAT THE FBI COULD USE. DIMITRI AND OTHER AGENTS ARE TO RETURN TO ISLAND. GRACE IS TO GO BACK TO TOWN AND CONTINUE MONITORING SHERIFF'S ACTIVITIES FOR 2 DAYS AND THEN RETURN TO ISLAND. SHE HAS A LOT TO EXPLAIN TO ME, EXPECIALLY WHY I'M GETTING THIS INFORMATION FROM THE MOLE AND NOT HER. SHE SHOULD HAVE HAD IT FIRST. I HAVE A SPECIAL ASSIGNMENT FOR GRACE AND DIMITRI WHEN THEY ARRIVE BACK HERE. NOW GET BUSY AND GET OUT OF THERE.

Sergei typed in: MESSAGE RECEIVED.

He pushed back his chair and rushed into the sleeping quarters, turning on a bright overhead light.

"Wake up, wake up now! We have to leave. The Major says the FBI and the sheriff will be at the house by 10:00. We've got a lot to do. Get up! Get dressed! Hurry! We don't have much time."

How did the Major get that information, Grace thought, and from whom? That proved to her that Vorack was right. There was a Russian mole in the FBI.

"Dimitri, the Major wants you to take Natasia, Maxim, and me back to the island," reported Sergei. "Grace is to go back to town and keep up her surveillance for another two days and then come to the island."

"Dimitri," Sergei continued, "He wants us to copy all our information onto discs and bring them with us. He wants the computers destroyed and anything else that could lead to him."

"OK," answered Dimitri. "You heard Sergei, get going— hurry! I'd like to be out of here in an hour."

"We're going to need more time. The download process is slow and cumbersome," Natasia pleaded.

"Just hurry, Natasia. Just hurry."

Grace was already back in the sleeping quarters looking through trash baskets and going through drawers. While checking the shower, she bent down to pull out hair caught in the drain. The shower rod and curtain fell on her and she wrestled to free herself from the bulky plastic.

"Damn," she cursed. "Isn't this hard enough?"

Almost everyone was packed up and out of the room. She gathered her personal items together and threw her backpack on her bed.

She could hear Dimitri and Sergei using sledge hammers to destroy the computers.

"Dimitri," Maxim yelled over the din.

Dimitri held up his hand for Sergei to stop.

"What do you think of burning the house down? Sure would make it harder for the Feds. They might think it was arson, some kids out for fun."

"Might work. Do we have enough kerosene?"

"I'll go look around."

"How's the download coming, Natasia?" Dimitri asked, "it's almost 8:00."

"This is the last one, almost done, fifteen minutes, tops."

It seems a shame to burn this place down, Grace thought. She remembered the elegant place settings and so many beautiful things still upstairs in the formal dining room. It had such a sense of history. She knew it was best to keep such thoughts to herself. Still, she felt that she was betraying the old house.

Maxim came back lugging five cans of kerosene. "Found some," he said proudly.

"Good work, Max," Dimitri said. "Natasia?"

"Done," answered Natasia. "It's all yours. Smash away."

"OK. We don't have a lot of fuel, but this place is old and dry except for the basement here, where it's a little damp and musty."

"Don't we know it, said Sergei sardonically. "We had to live with it for months."

"Well Sergei, now you'll have your revenge," Dimitri said. "Go up to the attic and start dumping out the kerosene. Max, you take the dining room upstairs. Grace, you and Natasia make sure to spread the kerosene around down here. When you're done, meet me by the front door. Here, let me soak this rag in it first. We need it to start the bonfire. Go."

Fifteen minutes later the five of them stood outside the front door.

"Are we sure we have everything we need? Everyone has checked? Nothing left behind? No? Ready?" asked Dimitri.

"Yes, yes," answered Sergei anxiously. "Just get on with it. I want to get out of here."

Dimitri took out his lighter and went up on the porch. He lit the rag and threw it through the front door, the room igniting like a torch.

"Run, Dimitri! Hurry! It could explode!"

Grace couldn't believe how fast the house started to burn. She could see flames leaping out of the attic window already. She reached down instinctively to touch her bracelet, only to find it gone. Oh God, she thought. It must have come off while she was working in the sleeping quarters. She remembered having it when she got in bed the night before. She was heartbroken.

The smoke filled the area as the flames reached the trees. A pair of mourning doves flew off frantically, fleeing their nest on one of the branches in a tall maple at the edge of the ravine in front of the house.

Reaching the iron gate, Grace looked back and saw a tall plume of black smoke rising high above the roof. The house started to collapse in on itself and black sooty ash began to fall, covering the pathway to the field below. She knew two people who were going to be very disappointed.

Thirty-two

"Quinn, Quinn, look up there, smoke," shouted Jake, driving the command vehicle in front of the convoy.

She picked up her binoculars and focused on the black sooty plume rising above the trees up toward the Ridge.

"Oh shit," she said and grabbed her phone. "Better get the copter up there," she said to Jake as she pressed a button on her phone. "Peterson, get Collins, take the helicopter, and head out over the Ridge to the Morefield House, or what might be left of it," she barked into the mouthpiece. "It looks like from here, someone's set it on fire!"

"Yes ma'am," Peterson replied. "I'll have Copter 2, follow with a water bucket."

"After you see what's up there, Peterson, circle the area and look for anyone on foot. Report back asap. We should be at house location in—"

She looked over at Jake.

"About an hour."

"We're estimating about an hour."

"Copy that. Over and out."

Quinn dropped the phone in her lap. "It sure doesn't look good, does it?"

"It sure doesn't."

Thirty-three

By 9 a.m., the sun shone brightly down on the town of Caswell Bay, briefly obscured by passing white billowy clouds. But at the Ridge, it seemed more like twilight. Thick smoke blocked out the sun's rays. Grace, Dimitri and the other agents were just below the path to the house, fleeing across the grassy meadow toward the safety of a stand of fir trees on the far perimeter. Feeling exposed in the open meadow, they increased their gait to a trot.

Sitting at a computer all day with little exercise left Sergei and his fellow agents out of breath. He hoped they could keep up the pace Dimitri had set for them. Natasia caught her foot on a tangle of vines and stumbled. Grace ran back and picked her up. Tightly holding Grace's arm, Natasia was able to keep in step with her despite the pain in her ankle. She kept looking ahead at the stand of trees now only fifty feet ahead.

Dimitri paused on the edge of the forest. Sweat

coursed down the side of his face. He glanced back over his shoulder at the rest of the group close behind and up at the thick smoke at the top of the ridge. The sky was clearer now and he could smell the fresh air at last. The rhythmic whup-whup sound of an approaching helicopter caught his attention.

"Faster everyone," he shouted. "Faster!"

They barely made it as the helicopter became visible. It crossed over the meadow and headed up toward the house. They watched it hover there for a few moments and then start sweeping the area again. They found a small group of boulders inside the thick trees and hid there until all was quiet again. Then they sighted another helicopter, a water bucket dangling below.

They continued on following the snakelike path through the shadowy canopy of trees leading back to town, constantly looking ahead to be sure they didn't run into the search party. A half hour later, they arrived at a point in the path where it split in two.

"This way," Dimitri called back to Grace. She'd stopped and sat on a boulder trying to remove a pebble from her shoe. When she reached down to retie her shoelace, she looked again in sadness at her empty wrist.

They headed north down the more traveled path toward the Bide a Wee cabins. The path was easy, fairly level until it made a sharp turn that headed back toward the Bay. There they parted.

"Remember, be at the island day after tomorrow," Dimitri admonished Grace. "The Major is already upset with you and you don't need to make it worse for herself."

"Don't worry," she snapped. "I'll be there. Kiss

the Major for me."

He gave her a dirty look. "That's a disgusting thought."

Dimitri continued on with the other agents, taking the path toward the secluded cabin Grace had stayed in when she first arrived. The area was deserted. They'd have a long wait until it got dark before moving toward Pickett's Point. Dimitri wondered if they'd all fit into the small motorboat. He checked his backpack to reassure himself he had brought the signaling device.

Meanwhile, Grace went on back to town by herself. She stopped and sat on a fallen tree trunk. She needed to think. She didn't know how long it would take Jake and the FBI to get back into town. She had to make a decision. She didn't trust Dimitri and she didn't know if the Major was angry enough to have her killed.

Grace had seldom been in as much danger. Vorack had to be stopped. She couldn't let him end the lives of hundreds of innocent people. She felt if she could tell Jake about her role in all of this, they could work together to bring down the Major. Jake needed to know everything. She only hoped Jake could forgive her for her deception. He'd have to realize the importance of the perilous role she'd been playing.

She looked up in the vivid blue sky and followed a single white billowy cloud as it drifted lazily by. It didn't seem to care that it was alone in the vast blue heaven. As Grace started back down the path, she didn't glance back. She knew that the cloud had probably vaporized. She didn't want to see that.

Looking back down the trail, Grace took in a

deep breath, rose, and adjusted the straps on her backpack. There was just one thing she had to do before she headed toward the beach house.

When she finally arrived, she went behind the house to his patio. She threw her backpack on the table, then sat in the swing chair. The ocean was calm. Closing her eyes, she drifted back to the happy times she'd shared with Jake, remembering the love they'd shared there. Daydreaming. She needed that. Storm clouds were just over the horizon.

Thirty-four

As Jake and Quinn waited for a report from the helicopter, Jake called Clyde over to take a look at the fire through his binoculars.

"What do you think, Clyde? It's coming from the Morefield House isn't it?"

"Yeah, has to be. It's concentrated in that one area. Hope it doesn't spread. I'd hate to get trapped in the middle of it."

"You're right, let's move out."

"Quinn, who could have told the bastards we were coming? By the time we get there, any clues will have gone up in smoke. Let's hope something's left in the rubble."

Quinn put up a hand as she spoke into her phone. "Yes Collins, yes."

She hung up, her face flushed. The phone call didn't make her happy.

"Sheriff, Collins reported that the house looked as if it was totally destroyed," she said, her expression grim. "What was left looked as if it's collapsed into the basement. The surrounding trees are still burning. I'm glad we brought the bulldozer. Now we're going to need it to clean up the debris. What we really need is a crane with a claw and a couple of dump trucks."

"Quinn, I can have one brought up from Farmsville," Jake said. "There's a building equipment supply store there. It'll take a couple of days to get one up here. I'll put a call in to Tina and have her order one. In the meantime, our only recourse is to shovel. Who knows, we may get lucky."

"Well, Sheriff, the good news is that the helicopter arrived a half hour ago with the water bucket. It's going to continue to wet down the house until the fire goes out to make it possible to at least get started looking through the debris. I told Collins to go back to base and fly us in some debris removal equipment, yeah, shovels and plastic bags. He can drop it close to the site. He said it'd take about an hour."

The agents nodded in agreement.

"We're almost there, Quinn. See, just over that rise ahead. We'll have to get the road cleared out. We're going to need parking spaces too. At least the smoke has dissipated. The water drop must be working."

The convoy stopped. They had to get the other vehicles off the road in order to bring up the bulldozer. Jake walked over with Quinn and leaned into the window of a jeep holding some of her agents.

"Could you men help getting these vehicles out

of the road?" he asked. "We need to bring up the bulldozer to clear a path into the house. It has to be wide so the crane will be able to come through it in a couple of days. Clyde said there are a few shovels in the truck bringing up the dozer. We want to carefully remove and bag the debris to see if anything can be found underneath. We can start with what we've got."

The agents nodded in agreement.

Jake looked over at Quinn. "Better tell the copter to hold off on the water now. We don't need a shower yet."

Quinn went about giving the men their orders.

Jake could hear the motor start up on the dozer as Ben backed it off of the trailer bed. Dirt and rocks flew in all directions as the road smoothed and widened. Jake knew Ben had driven one working on the farm where he grew up. Ben was not only happy, but eager to accept the assignment and smiled at Jake as the chugging dozer passed by.

Ben looked down. "How am I doing, Chief?"

"A-1, Ben, just don't hit my car."

All the agents were out of their cars and had followed the bulldozer as if it were the Pied Piper. When they reached Jake and Agent Quinn, they gathered around awaiting further orders.

"OK men, and ladies, here's the plan," Jake began. "Ben should be finished soon with opening an entry into the crime scene. And that's what we're calling it, so you understand the importance of noticing everything. I want you to call our attention to anything you think pertains to the discovery of how this came to be or who's responsible. Hopefully, we'll be able to find something in the rubble. Usually, I'd say disturb nothing. In this case, since we have a time constraint that calls for immediate answers, we'll be digging into the debris. It's gonna be messy and smelly. Some of you have experience in fire cases. Normally too, the fire department would be involved. We've asked them to send a deputy up here. That's all we've requested for the time being and they're complying."

"Special Agent Quinn and I will review the crime scene first— alone. We'll then come back and ask for your assistance. Feel free to relax, have a drink of water, or whatever you want to do. Stay here. We'll be back shortly."

Thirty-five

Jake and Agent Quinn made their way through an opening in the bent and broken remains of the prickly rose bushes blocking the road. Behind them, the loud groaning sound of the bulldozer broke the silence that normally surrounded the once grand house. Jake was moved when he saw the charred remains that lay in front of them. He was happy he'd taken a Saturday a couple of months ago to come up and see it. Clyde had been right. It was spooky. But it must have been something in its glory days.

The pungent smell of burned wood filled their nostrils and penetrated their clothing. As Jake scanned the scene, it appeared as described. Almost all of the house had disappeared into a pile of rubble. The only thing left standing beside the massive brick chimney was part of the back entry and a boarded up in-ground set of doors. As he went to study that area more closely, Agent Quinn walked around to what had been the front of the house where a wide porch had in the past offered a view of the endless ocean.

Jake walked slowly around the back of the house, stopped, bent down and put on his latex gloves. He reached forward letting his hand hover above the plank of wood he was about to move. It felt warm. He pulled out his revolver and with the butt of the gun pushed at a charred board. It immediately crumbled into ashes.

Quinn came up behind him. He turned and looked up at her.

"Find anything?" Jake asked her.

"It looks as if the fire was started up front. They'd had to have used an accelerant. Everything there burned quickly. Not as bad back here though— what are you doing?"

"I was curious. See, in the ground here? I remembered there was a boarded up storm cellar. It's my guess, we'll find two doors that open up to the side under this debris. There must be stairs underneath, maybe still intact. Hopefully we'll be able to access the basement from here."

Jake knelt down again to examine the entranceway. "I left my phone in the car, Agent Quinn," he said, glancing up at her. "Can you call one of your men and bring me a shovel? A broom would be great too."

Quinn put in a call to Knox who arrived a few moments later with a shovel and handed it to Jake.

"No one could find a broom. All we could find was this whisk broom from one of the cars. Will it do?" he asked handing the tools to Jake.

"Thanks, Knox. See if you can pull away these other boards. I don't think they're hot. Be careful."

As Knox pulled off the boards, Jake could see the one on the bottom hardly burned.

"Wait," Jake said. "Hold it."

He pushed aside the last board, revealing the remains of a latch.

"I think this is one of the doors. Hand me the shovel."

Jake took the pointed end of the shovel's bowl and levered it into a crack where the board ended. Then he pried the door open. It came off with such force that Jake fell backward into Knox's arms.

"Gotcha, Sheriff," Knox laughed. "You don't know your own strength."

"Thanks." Back on his feet again, Jake stared into the gaping dark hole revealed by the missing door. He squatted down and took his flashlight and shined it inside. They all bent down and saw a flight of crumbling cement stairs, untouched by the fire, leading down into the basement.

"Jake," Quinn began. "I know what you're thinking. Don't go down there. It's too risky. The whole mess could fall down on you."

"Yeah, but I'm a need-to-know guy. Don't follow me. I'll call back and let you know how things are going."

"Jake, don't."

"Sorry." Jake disappeared down the stairs. They bent down further and could just make out his body silhouetted in the glow of his flashlight.

"What are you seeing down there, Sheriff?" Quinn called down to him.

"It's good news. Some of the basement isn't full of debris. There's a huge charred beam holding back whatever's above it. Looks like there's over half the room intact. It must have been sleeping quarters for whoever was here. I count three frame beds and what looks like a shower stall in the corner. There's water on the floor and everything looks sooty. If we're careful, we might be able to shore it up even more and do a thorough search. I'm going to look around a little more and then come back. So far, so

147

good."

"Be careful," Quinn yelled down. "Don't move anything for heaven's sake."

"I promise, Mom," Jake called back.

Jake moved carefully through the room, shining his light under and around anything he saw. Ankle deep water covered the floor. He constantly looked up and listened for any sound of shifting from the debris above him. He slogged over to the shower stall and pulled a soggy shower curtain out of the way to look inside. Shining his light around, he spotted something shiny in the water. He bent down and pulled it free. Jake stared in disbelief— It was a bracelet, a bracelet made up of tiny stars—Grace's bracelet!

"Jake, Jake, you OK?"

Quinn's voice snapped him out of his brain freeze.

"Yeah, uh, yes. Yes, I'm coming back now. Be right there." He took a small plastic bag from his pants pocket, slipped the bracelet inside it, zipped it tight and pushed the bag down as far as it would go into his pocket.

"Well, was it worth the risk, Jake?" Quinn asked as he cleared the stairs and gulped a breath of fresh air.

"I'd say so," he gasped. "Has the equipment arrived?"

"Yes. And Ben is done bulldozing. You ready to go back?"

"Let's go get everyone started. I have a feeling that by the end of the day, we're going to know a lot more than we know at the moment."

Thirty-six

Major Vorack sat in his office on Fisher Island awaiting the arrival of Dimitri and the three other agents. He hated to have communications cut off for even a moment. However, he quickly found a new location suitable for his communication center. An abandoned light house would have to suit the agents for the time being and Crook Neck Island was only one half mile from Fisher Island. It wouldn't be as comfortable, but that didn't matter. They wouldn't be there long.

He thought the idea of burning down the Morefield House and all its content was brilliant. He wished he could take credit for it. Dimitri told him it was Sergei's idea. What a surprise. He looked at the three agents as disposable when the mission was over. But then, he had more things to think about at the moment. One of them was Grace Cooper. He looked forward to seeing her in two days. He had plans for her as well.

As Vorack sat at his desk, he found himself staring down at two cylinders holding his spybirds, each fitted with a small vial of toxin, two of his best accomplishments. He found it easy to give himself

149

full credit. Yuri Petrenko, who spent several years developing the toxin and designing his spybirds was, of course, necessary.

He thought back on his early days in the KGB working with Colonel Trelenko. The Colonel trusted him. The Russian government trusted him. They loved his idea of the creation of the spybirds as well as setting up the lab right under the American's noses. It had taken some time to find the perfect location and hasn't that worked out well. Trelenko was the perfect go-between. He could be easily manipulated. Vorack found it wasn't hard to deceive everyone while still reciving financial backing for all these years. And to his delight, no one in the government had suspected the change in direction that he had secretly embarked on.

Vorack ran his hand over the shiny silver metallic cylinders, each light enough to carry in one hand, yet lethal enough to wipe out an entire city. He thought to himself, I'll be so rich in a few days and all thanks to you, my little ones He carried the cylinders out of the lab, the twins taking a much deserved nap inside their shiny tubes.

The other techs were too busy looking at their computer screens to notice him. He punched in a code on the wall sensor and the steel door slid open. The guard outside was engrossed in a conversation with the tech from the 2nd floor. Recognizing the Major, he snapped to attention as Vorack descended the stairs to the lowest section of the complex.

At the end of the corridor there was another thick grey steel door. Using a visual scanner, the Major placed his chin on the pad and stared into the small opening. His retina was detected and scanned. The door immediately slid open.

Inside, shelving lined walls that stretched for one hundred feet. A brightly lit ceiling loomed thirty feet above. Every shelf was filled with cylinders, clones of the ones the Major carried lovingly in his hands. His workers had done a remarkable job in the last two months. He gently placed them back in the rack where they came from and patted them with parental gentleness. "Soon, my baby birds, soon." As he left the room, the door silently slid closed.

Thirty-seven

When Jake left, the search team was knee-deep in rubble. They worked carefully, trying to remove the debris layer by layer. The constant threat of total collapse into the lower interior of the house, made everyone uneasy. Two oaks had been cut down to size and installed in the basement to create supports for the dangerously sagging ceiling.

Jake hurried back to his office to make his report, but his mind was filled with questions he had for Grace. The longer he kept the evidence, the more he felt responsible for jeopardizing the operation. Jake had a hard time believing Grace was a Russian spy, despite the evidence. He wanted to hear it from her. He wanted her to confess to him.

Once Quinn found out that she was a spy, she'd arrest her. His heart sank thinking of not having Grace in his life.

He closed his eyes and tried to remember what

made Grace so important to him. Physical attraction had drawn him toward her at first, but then as he came to know her, he saw her as strong, intelligent, and even funny at times. He felt comfortable talking together, confiding in her.

He'd wanted the new relationship to last. She led him to believe she cared a lot for him too. In fact, she'd told him that she felt she was falling in love with him. Perhaps that's why he missed recognizing the other Grace, the secret Grace. The bottom line? He wasn't ready to give up on her. But, he had to confront her— and soon.

Once back in his office, he dialed the 4-Poster.

"Hi Marge, this is Jake. Has Grace come back yet?"

"Oh, hi there Jake. What was all that smoke about up on the Ridge? Everyone's asking about it. Anything to do with that old Morefield House?"

"Yeah, it was the house."

"Well, it surprises me it lasted this long. Arson, you think? Kids, maybe? Why didn't the fire trucks go up, never heard a siren."

"Marge, we don't know yet. I'll let you know. Now, about Grace. Have you seen her?"

"Can't say that I have, Jake. Shall I go take another look?"

"No. It's alright. When she comes in, would you have her call me?"

"Sure thing."

Jake hung up. It was almost 6:00. Clyde and the rest of the agents should be coming back soon, he thought. Everyone had to be exhausted. Clyde needed to be told about Grace. Jake's clothes were still sooty and he still smelled like a campfire. He

153

decided to go home and clean up first and then get with Clyde later.

"Tina," he said, "I'm heading out to the beach house. I know it's late, but I'd appreciate it if you wait for Clyde. He should be here soon. Tell him I'm going to call him later. I need to talk with him. I think the FBI agents were going to head back to their motor homes. We're all going to meet here in the morning about 7:00."

"Yeah, Jake. You've had a tough day and look it. Go take a shower and get something to eat. You'll feel a lot better. See you in the morning."

"Thanks, Tina."

As Jake slid into his cruiser, his car phone started to ring. He picked it up. Before he could answer, he heard Grace's voice.

"Jake, are you back from the Ridge yet?"

"Grace? Where are you?"

"I'm sitting on the patio at your beach house. I've been here most of the day waiting for you to come back. It's getting a little chilly."

"What? I'm headed there right now," Jake said, forcing himself to remain calm. "Go around to the front door. You'll see a pile of rocks off to the right. There's a white heart-shaped stone near the base. There's a key under the rock. Let yourself in. I should be there in about fifteen minutes."

"I won't leave, Jake. I've got a lot to tell you."

Thirty-eight

Grace found the key before they finished talking. As the screen door banged shut behind her she stood in the entry and let her eyes slowly roam through the living room, replaying scenes from her last visit to Jake's home.

She threw her backpack down on the floor by the door. Grace went into the kitchen and fixed herself a glass of pinot grigio and poured another for Jake. He'd need it. She hoped she could salvage their relationship. She wanted him in her life. If they could only get through the next few days, maybe they could start over.

She took out her cell phone and waited for someone to answer her expected call. After repeating the appropriate series of words, she told the listener, "I put the information in a manila envelope. There's a dumpster behind the Hungry Goose diner. Yes. Look for it there." She put the glass of wine to her lips and let the cool liquid slide slowly down her throat.

As she fell back into his favorite overstuffed easy

chair, her eyes turned toward the small framed picture on the end table next to her. There, a photograph of a smiling, cuddling Jake and Grace looked back at her. She remembered they'd just been out for a sail on the bay—a beautiful day, wind blowing in her hair and Jake looking so sexy standing at the wheel of the boat. Jake and Grace. She liked the sound of that.

She turned her head to see Jake's cruiser pull into the driveway. As he started up the walk, she could see he'd come from the site of the fire. His uniform was covered with dark sooty stains and he looked tired.

She stood as he entered, her arm outstretched, offering him the drink she'd fixed for him. He motioned her to sit down, but took the drink. He finished it in one swallow.

"Stay there, Grace. I need another one. You?"

She nodded.

When Jake came back, he handed one of the glasses of wine to Grace and sat down on the couch facing her.

"Drink up," he said looking straight at her with a cop's stare. He reached into his pocket and pulled out a piece of paper and a small plastic bag. He placed the paper where she could read the now visible word, "Vorack!" He dumped the contents of the small bag on the coffee table in front of her.

"My bracelet," she gasped as she snatched it up off the table. "Where did you—" Realization dawned in her features, her voice trailing off at the sight of the penciled-over paper. "Oh, my God. Jake, wait, I can explain."

Grace's eyes welled up with tears.

Jake sat rigid and unblinking.

"That's why I'm here," Grace pleaded breathlessly. "Be patient with me, there's so much."

Part of him wanted to console her. The other part stayed protected, coldly removed, professional, waiting.

"Let's hear it," Jake said.

She reached into her pocket and pulled out a tissue.

"Jake, this isn't easy for me. Just wait until I tell you the whole story before you ask any questions."

He nodded.

"I am a double agent," Grace said. She took a deep breath and continued. I'm working for both the Russian government and the United States."

"What?"

"Please wait, Jake. Please."

He listened as Grace told him how she was recruited and trained.

"After college, I thought it'd be exciting to have a career in law enforcement. I was accepted by the FBI. A few years ago, I was sent to Russia by the the Bureaul to try and find out what had happened to Major Anton Vorack. I speak Russian fluently. Before I left, I was given extensive training by the FBI in code breaking. I had a cover job inside our embassy in the cipher department.

"The FBI had contacts deep inside the Russian government leading to my recruitment a few months later by a Major Trelenko. I was sent back here to the US and stationed in Boston by Trelenko . I was to await orders on a mission involving Major Vorack. Ironic, don't you think? The FBI was delighted. Ever since my joining up with Vorack,

I've been giving the FBI information. The Russians recruited me while I was really a spy for the US. They set me up to work with Vorack and I've been giving the FBI information about him and his operation on Fisher Island. The FBI wanted me to get in contact with you pretending to be a tourist, but not to give you any information about the mission."

"So you used me to get information for both sides?" Jake asked coldly.

"Yes—yes and no," Grace said. "I mean, that's how our relationship began. Then I got to know you and— I'm so sorry."

She rose to go over to him.

"Not yet." He shook his head. "Sit back down and tell me the rest, Grace."

"Well, I was supposed stay put at the 4-Poster and wait to be contacted by Vorack's team," she said, looking into his eyes. "I was also to find out about anything suspicious going on that could point the Feds in his direction. That's how you caught me headed out to the island that day. I really was checking out the report of the flashing lights. Of course I know the answer to that now. I kept in contact with the FBI by cell phone using a code, feeding the Agency the info about what I'd found out. I was told they didn't want to move in until I discovered what Vorack was planning to do and when."

Grace got up and went over and picked up her backpack. Digging deep inside she pulled out a thick manila file. She placed it on the coffee table between them and opened it up to a page halfway through the stack of papers inside. Then, she handed it to Jake.

"Here Jake, you read the rest yourself. You know

most of it by now anyway. I'm going to step outside for a few minutes. I need some air. I promise I'll be back in."

Jake stood at the front window looking outside. He watched a single seagull circling above the house. Suddenly it swooped down low headed toward the beach.

He turned around at the sound of Grace re-entering the house. When Grace returned to the living room, she saw the closed folder laying on the coffee table. They both sat back down across from one another.

"I wanted to tell you all this right after I got to know you," she said. "The Director wouldn't allow it. I don't care what he thinks now. I want you with me."

"Bear with me, Grace," Jake said in a slow voice. "I'm still overwhelmed by all of this. Think of it this way. One day we're dating, having fun, falling in love and the next day, you're a double agent for the government." He shook his head. "I just can't believe why I didn't catch on earlier. I have to say though, you're an amazing woman. Grace, at least I now understand why your behavior left me wondering about you. I even worried that you might even be seeing someone else, or had a husband hidden away. Your sudden, unexplained departures made me angry. Hey, I'm a detective. I needed to know what was going on."

"So you were jealous, Jake?" Grace smiled for the first time since Jake had arrived. "Look Jake, I'm still the same Grace you enjoyed being with. This is just another facet of who I am. Can you let yourself remember that woman you kissed on the Ferris wheel?"

Jake looked across at Grace for a moment that seemed to last a lifetime to Grace. Then he rose and walked over to her and took her hands in his.

"You know, you take my breath away," he said. "You're brave, intelligent, strong, passionate. You're quite a woman, Grace Cooper. Look, let's try and get through the next few days. The rest we'll work out together later."

Grace put her arms around Jake. He tilted her head up toward his and once more looked down into those wondrous green eyes. Nothing mattered except the moment they were sharing. She was an extraordinary woman.

"I love you, Jake. Don't ever leave me."

Thirty-nine

As the last of the setting sun moved through the bedroom window, Jake took his hand and gently smoothed Grace's hair away from her face.

"Grace, Grace, I missed you so much."

She smiled at Jake and ran her hands across his wet bare chest. He didn't want the moment to end. They lay silently cuddled like two spoons in a drawer, sinking deeply into the down comforter on Jake's bed. Moving slowly away, Jake sat up and took a sip of wine and closed his eyes, savoring the moment. How cool and sweet it tasted. Putting his glass back on the nightstand, Jake lay down and pulled Grace toward him again.

"One more time."

She smiled and put her arms around his waist and yielded to his desire for her and hers for him. She closed her eyes, drifting off into blessed sleep. It was as if she were in a dream, a fairy tale where the two of them would live happily ever after.

An hour later, Grace awoke in the dark, and she knew the nightmare was yet to begin.

Grace slipped into the shower, then returned to look down at Jake. He was still asleep, worn out from stress and the evening of intimacy. She bent over him and kissed him lightly on his forehead. He awoke with a start.

"It's OK." She slipped back in bed beside him and whispered, "It's only the woman who comes here to sleep with you."

He laughed and embraced her. "You're a dangerous woman, Grace Cooper. I love you. I want to be with you, I want to wake up every morning and see you next to—"

Grace put her two fingers across Jake's lips. She had to stop the words from coming.

"I love you too, Jake Mason," she said, her breath sweet against his face. "I want you to say that to me again after all this is over. I've always been afraid to plan my future beyond the mission I had to complete. I never really knew if there would be a future for me. I can tell you right now, I want to wake up next to you every morning too. But before that, I have to complete the mission. That means going back to the island tonight. This time, I promise to keep in touch with you."

"Tonight? No. When?"

"11:15. What time is it?"

"It's 10:30," Jake answered pulling her closer to him. "You know if I had a choice, you wouldn't be going. It's so dangerous. How do you do it? You put your life on the line every time you go out to the island."

She turned facing him. "And you, Jake, when you were working in Los Angeles? Were you in danger often?" She had him there. "We chose what we wanted to do with our lives. For me, I thought it'd be exciting and I'd get to travel. Silly, right? I was just a kid. I can't say it wasn't exciting living on the edge for the first few years." Her face hardened. Grace looked as if she was remembering things she wanted to forget. "But Jake, living each day as if it might be your last; putting your life in the hands of our nation's enemies—it grows old."

She raised herself up on one elbow and looked directly into his eyes. "We're so close to getting the Major and ending his career once and for all. I won't back away. It's not in my nature. We'll get this monster. But, I've decided that when this mission is over, Director Thompson and I are going to have a talk. He won't be happy. I feel ready to resign. I'd like a more predictable normal life, if there is such a thing," she said laughingly lying back down against his warm body. "I'd like a husband and a family. And here you are. It makes me think that might be possible. I guess the turning point for me was finding someone to love and who loved me back."

Jake reached over and brushed back several strands of her hair. "Let's talk about it after the mission. I'll back whatever decision you want to make. Let's enjoy the time we have together," Jake said. He kissed her. "I'm here for the duration."

They rose and stood beside the bed holding each other tightly, not wanting to let go. She looked up at him. "Come on, let's go out on the patio, snuggle up, and look at the stars."

Just beyond the flagstone patio on the beach, they sat down in the wooden glider. It slowly moved back and forth with the two of them wrapped snugly together in the down comforter from the bed. Grace could feel the cool sand between her bare toes. She loved that feeling.

The moon, low on the horizon, no longer blocked the view of the stars that seemed to go on forever. The outline of Fisher Island was barely recognizable but for the blinking of the warning buoy at the opening to the harbor. The lighthouse sent out its warning beam toward Crook Neck Island.

The day had been so hot, but now there was a cooling onshore breeze. The flagpole halyard tapped out a soft rhythmic metallic beat as the wind slapped it against the pole. The seabirds had settled in for the night in a rookery a half mile from the house. All was calm. Jake took a deep breath and inhaled the salty scent of the sea.

Better snap out of it, he thought, considering the day that lay ahead. He looked at Grace. Her eyes were closed. He wondered where she was.

He reached over and touched her arm. She gave a slight jerk and opened her eyes.

"Grace, It's time."

"Don't get up, Jake," she said as she slid out of the blanket and stood up. "Stay here and pretend I'm still next to you. I will call you. Promise."

She bent down and gave Jake a kiss. He pulled her back down and kissed her again before letting her go.

"Love you," he whispered. "Be safe, please. See you soon."

"Love you too."

Jake looked back up into the heavens. A 'shooting star' arced halfway between the Orion constellation and the faint outline of Fisher Island visible against the horizon. Maybe that'll bring us good luck, he mused. We can sure use some of that.

He was lost in the beauty of the night and never heard the screen door closing softly behind him.

Forty

Grace looked at her watch, 11:15.

Leaving the beach house, flashlight in hand, she made her way along the dark path behind Jake's cottage curving to the left and then merging with the path that lead down to the shoreline. She was happy she'd worn long jeans as the sharp thistles, tangled and bent, narrowed the passageway. She followed the beach toward town. Beyond the marina, she went up the stairs leading to the sidewalk in front of Tinker's Hardware. It took her another few minutes to make her way to Pickett's Point. The small boat they kept for travel back and forth to the island was safely anchored in the tall reeds at the foot of a hill, not visible from land or sea.

When she reached the boat, she took a cylindrical device out of her small overnight bag. When she turned it on, it produced a red beam strong enough to be seen from Fisher Island. Aiming it toward the south end of the island, she hit the on button three times in succession and then once more. She waited and watched. About a minute later, a small blue beam returned her signal, on and off, on and off.

She got in and pushed away from the shore. The sea was getting choppy. She could see lightning on the horizon, signaling a nasty incoming storm. She pushed the throttle forward and headed the boat toward the hidden opening on Fisher Island. But her heart wasn't in it. She knew they'd be waiting for her. She wasn't looking forward to what she'd encounter when she got inside. She definitely wasn't looking forward to meeting up again with the maniac Major.

Meanwhile, Vorack anticipated her return eagerly. He was delighted that he'd be off the cursed island in four days. He longed to see the sunshine and see other people, men and women who didn't dress in white coats always needing something. He'd been patient, but wanted some semblance of his old life back. But soon he'd be able to live it in style. He'd put in a request to have the freighter, *Levongrad* show up at 2 a.m. Sunday morning. The weather forecast was for a nasty storm tonight, but promised a cloud overcast for the rendezvous. There would be no moon to light up the water either. Perfect, he thought.

The cylinders with the skybirds safely inside would already be securely loaded into padded boxes for transport to the ship. The transfer should take two hours max. He'd have men with machine guns posted on the perimeter of the island to intercept any interference from an unexpected occurrence.

The FBI had moved faster than he'd expected. He'd barely been able to warn the Morefield House team. He'd try to think of a plan to divert their attention away from the island area.

He'd told his trusted worker, Petrov, to plant

small explosives throughout the three floors of the underground building. Petrov would stay behind and detonate them after he reached a safe distance from the island. Fireworks on Sunday night? Why wait? He'd show them some fireworks.

He'd arranged with the Captain of the *Levongrad* to deliver half the expected cargo to the government agency. The loss of the other half of the boxes would be explained as an accident in transfer to the ship. In actuality, they were headed to a warehouse where the contents would be sold to the highest bidder. Right now, Turkey and Iran were at the top of the list. The Captain and his selected crew had been paid well for their silence.

His plan was to rendezvous with the magnificent *Miscovic* submarine even before the transfer was complete. There, he'd be safe with his own little nest of birds. His insurance he called it. He'd have the ten boxes in case something went wrong. In fact, he already had the boxes with their cylinders containing their lethal toxin packed up and hidden ready to load into his escape boat Sunday morning. Only he and Petrov knew of his plan. Yes, a great plan. So, what could go wrong?

His workers would be the last to leave the island, followed by the security force. As for Yuri Petrenko and his lab assistants? The Major smiled. In military terms, the white-coated drones would be "wastage," unfortunate casualties. Their usefulness to him would be over. He wanted to get rid of anyone who might compromise his plans. Petrenko would know he was expendable—and that the major hated him— so he had to go. Dimitri and Grace? They'd be too much of a threat. He had his plan for them too.

Dimitri was already below in the commissary and Grace was expected in one half hour.

After the explosion, there'd be a lot of confusion. Even the FBI would take a while to figure out what to do. In the beginning, they'd be more focused on the debris and casualties left by the explosion. Darkness would hinder their efforts. So time would be on his side. They'd probably send up a helicopter, but he'd be safely on board the sub and miles away from the area by then. They'd probably spot the *Levongrad*. But the captain and crew having been paid well, would keep quiet. The Captain had orders to dump the cargo if they got too close. Sure, the government would lose its cargo, but they won't find him. He laughed. Life will be good. He was sure of it.

"Major, sorry to bother you." Boris appeared in the doorway. "Grace Cooper just returned to the base?"

"Did you talk to her?"

"Yes. She asked for Dimitri."

"Where is Dimitri?"

"I don't know. I—" He never finished the sentence.

Vorack was on his feet and out the door. He went down the hall, Boris at his heels, and entered a small security room. "I want you to find Grace and Dimitri. Now!"

Scanning the bank of screens, the technician pointed to the left.

"There they are, Major. Look, near his quarters. They, they're just standing there talking."

"Good work, Boris. Retrieve them and bring them to my office. Quickly now."

When Grace saw Boris coming down the stairs, she swore under her breath. The Major had found them. Boris motioned for them to follow him.

"The Major wants to see you."

Grace pushed her hand into her pocket and wrapped her hand around the small pistol still hidden there. She knew the Major was angry with her and that didn't bode well.

Forty-one

Major Vorack's office was well lit. He was playing one of his favorite folk recordings from his boyhood in Lestovia. While he had worked so hard to Americanize and blend in, his heart was still back home in his mother country. He had a bottle of Stoli vodka and three glasses brought in. After all, this was a celebration.

"Welcome. I am so happy you've returned to our little home away from home."

Dimitri grimaced. What was the old psycho up to now?

Grace was surprised. Not at all what she'd expected. She couldn't trust his mood swings and only took her hand out of her pocket, when he offered her a drink.

"You two are just the ones I wanted to see. Sit down. Here. Have a toast to Mother Russia.

They downed their glasses. Vorack refilled them.

171

"And to the near completion of our work here. You two have been very helpful. Drink, drink." He held his glass high and drank it down in one gulp.

"We'll be going home in four days! Before we leave, I have one last mission for you to accomplish. I am going to tell you why we have set up this facility. I, with the assistance of Dr. Petrenko, have designed a device that flies, undetectable, through the air and can carry and dispense a lethal toxin capable of poisoning thousands of people. And that is just one of its capabilities."

"But why wouldn't it be seen and disarmed or shot down?" Dimitri interjected.

"Why, it can be made invisible. No one will see it coming," Vorack answered.

"Yes, sir. Right you are," answered Dimitri glancing over at the Grace's poker face. "You are really clever, Major."

"Why, thank you Dimitri. No comment from you, Grace?"

"Indeed, Major," Grace said. She was stunned. "An amazing accomplishment."

"Thank you, my dear. And because the two of you are so special, I am going to give you one of the cylinders, fully ready to do its job. Tomorrow, the two of you are to go to New Barnum and release it in the reservoir. You'll be fully trained as to how to accomplish this, not to worry. There will be no failure."

The Major explained that Dimitri and Grace would leave at dawn. They were to drive to a predetermined launch site and, at exactly 10 a.m., open the cylinder and activate his spybird. When airborne, it would automatically release the toxin over the water.

"The payload should have reached its maximum potential for dispersal of the toxin in the water and people will have it coming out of their faucets, the reservoir being small, in about 12 hours later. I am not making the drug lethal for the test. There would be too much attention and annoying authorities coming into the area. There'll be plenty of activity at the area hospitals though. I expect many, many nauseated people."

Dimitri smelled a rat. Why carry out a test that would only bring attention to the mission without doing any real damage to the enemy? And why was the Major taking them into his confidence? He never told people the why of anything, he just ordered it done.

"Bring the cylinder back to me here," Vorack said. "I expect you to be in this room by 6:00 tomorrow evening."

"Major—" Grace began.

"I'm not done yet," he sneered. "This must, and I emphasize must, be done without any mistakes. Mark my words, none." He turned on Grace. "You already bungled your first job, keeping us a step ahead of the FBI; now don't screw this one up." He stood and looked down at the two agents. "There will be dire consequences for you both, if something were to go wrong. I am sending Boris along with you to make sure all goes well."

Grace felt the hair rise on her arms. Now she understood. They'd do their job and Boris would do his. They weren't coming back from this one. This can't happen, she thought. She had to find a way to call Jake before they left in the morning. But how?

"Now I want you to put your cell phones and any weapons you have with you, on my desk. You won't need them."

"But we'll need to communicate with you."

"No, Boris will send me a message at the completion of the mission. I've set up your fellow comrades on Crook Neck Island in the abandoned lighthouse to receive messages." He sat down and began shuffling papers; a signal that the meeting was at an end—no questions. He looked back up at them. "Boris knows how to do that. Valeria is coming to take you to the lab and meet with Dr. Petrenko. He'll show you how to use the cylinders. You'll be leaving first thing in the morning."

Reluctantly, Grace and Dimitri left with their escort.

Forty-two

After the briefing, Valeria wished them a good mission and escorted Dr. Petrenko back to his lab. After they were out of sight, Grace pulled Dimitri into a blind spot out of view of the security camera and whispered in his ear.

"Meet me in the women's room on Level 2 in five minutes. Be cautious. Make sure you're not followed and don't look into any cameras. No one can see us inside that area. I'll be sure it's empty. Now, smile. Don't look so tense. We're supposed to be happy. Remember?"

Two minutes later, right on cue, Dimitri opened the women's restroom door. Grace brushed past him and locked the door. She leaned up against it as if her body could prevent any intruder from stopping her from this mission.

"We're in a lot of trouble. You know what the maniac's intentions are don't you, Grace? If I could figure out a way to kill him, I would."

"I have a plan" she responded. "I have to get to Petrenko and talk to him. I was able to get his lab code. I don't have time to go into it with you, but he can help us and we can help him in return. Valeria will be watching the security monitors tonight. You two are friends, are you not?"

He smiled.

"See if you can distract her so she doesn't see me talking to Petrenko. If I can get him into a safe place for a few moments, hopefully she won't see he's missing from her view. I just need ten minutes."

"Ten minutes! That's a lot of distraction."

"You'll think of something. Now hurry. I need to find Petrenko. You go to see her tonight at 7 p.m. Wish me luck."

Dr. Petrenko, now back in his office on Level 2, was alone, deep in thought working late. He didn't hear the door open. Grace scanned the room and saw the camera placement. She looked at her watch. 7:00 exactly. I hope you're where you're supposed to be Dimitri, she thought, and walked close to the wall and under the camera.

Petrenko looked up at his computer screen catching an image of someone silently moving behind him. Picking up a letter opener on his desk, he swirled around and started to say something and saw Grace. She put her fingers to her lips.

"Turn around and keep working," she said. "I want to talk to you. In a minute, slowly get up and join me here away from the camera. Don't be alarmed. I've got this covered."

Petrenko turned and continued as if nothing happened. Then got up and casually made his way to where she stood.

"I'll try to make this as quick as possible. We only have ten minutes."

Petrenko started to say something and she stopped him again. "Just listen for now."

She told him about the Major's plans and asked for his help. In return, she'd make it possible for him to escape the island. She asked him to switch vials on the Major, so that she and Dimitri would have one without toxin.

The exchange between them didn't take long and he reluctantly agreed to help her.

She looked at her watch again, 7:08.

"I have to go now. Be safe, doctor. You have to trust me."

Petrenko picked up a manual just in case they were watching again, went back to his work at the table. He thought, how in hell can I trust this woman I've met only briefly. She comes in here, at great peril to us both, proposes this dangerous switch of the toxin in ten minutes, and wants me to go along with it?

He mulled over the information she'd given him. He might be able to pull it off.

Years ago when he first started working on these deadly inventions, they told him either work with them or they'd find someone who would. He knew what that meant and chose life over death. Later, he berated himself for being weak. What was one life worth when compared with so many innocents? He'd struggled with that decision ever since.

Now, knowing Vorack being more evil than he could ever have imagined, it was an empty choice. His chances of leaving this place alive were pretty slim. His life underground had been like prison. For a month now, he'd been trying to discover a way to sabotage the results and not get caught, but nothing yet. So what did he have to lose? If Grace had an escape plan that works, there could be a slim chance he might even get out of this alive. He'd be seeing her for the switch. He hoped the plan sounded doable.

Even with all the security on the island, they'd become lax lately and that would help. He had made friends with a guard, Ilya Kostalow, who was also interested in science. Petrenko and Ilya had long conversations about Ilia's ambitions to leave this job and better himself. He wanted to defect and become a science teacher. Maybe, just maybe, Ilya would look the other way when the time came. This could be his backup plan.

Forty-three

Jake hadn't slept much Wednesday night. He worried about Grace; he hadn't heard from her yet.

When he arrived at the department, he saw Agent Quinn's van parked near the front door. She knew he'd wanted to meet with her and got there early. Grace had called Quinn last night before she left for the island and told her Jake was in. He'd agreed their joint effort would certainly lead to the successful capture of the Major. Quinn was good with the information being shared. "Makes the team stronger," she had said.

Grace told her to tell Jake that all her FBI agents would fully cooperate in whatever decision he made. It was his town. He knew it best. With Summerfair being set up on Friday, they had to move quickly and efficiently.

Jake headed for his office. Clyde was already there waiting for him.

"You OK, Jake?" Clyde asked. "What's up?"

"Hang on a minute. I want Agent Quinn in here with us," Jake said, going back into the squad room. It was quickly filling as the agents went about their assigned duties. Quinn was talking with Cortes and looked up as Jake approached.

"Sheriff, I want to talk to you," she said.

"Great minds think alike, Agent Quinn," Jake smiled. "I've been looking for you, too. If you've got a moment, come into my office. We can talk there."

After Quinn was seated, he asked her, "Have you talked to Grace recently?"

"Yes, she called me last night after she left your place. I'm aware of your conversation."

"Good, that will help."

Clyde interrupted, "Grace? What's she got to do with any of this?"

"Agent Quinn, I want to bring Clyde in on this. He and I have worked as a team since I've arrived. He'd be a big help. I trust him implicitly. This information won't leave this room, until I get your OK. What do you say?"

"Could I talk to you privately Sheriff?" she said.

Before Jake could answer, Clyde said amiably "Hey, it's OK, I need a cup of coffee anyway.

How about you guys?"

"As black as midnight," Quinn spoke up.

"You know my poison, Clyde."

"Thanks, buddy, won't be a moment," Jake said as he closed the door to his office and returned to his desk.

Quinn shifted in her seat. "Sheriff, I respect your judgement and at first blush I'd have no problem with your deputy being fully apprised of what's going on," she said. "But here's the deal. In time, Grace's role as an agent of our government will be made public. Right now we don't want to reveal her identity, for obvious reasons. We want to keep her as safe as possible."

So do I, Jake thought. So do I. His mind flashed to the rocky slopes of Fisher Island and Grace entombed in its forbidding walls.

"On the other hand, we've put in a number of years training her as a Russian mole," Quinn continued. "We may need her in the future. Of course, she'd have to change her identity and appearance, but she's a valuable asset. As I said, I trust your judgment—and Clyde's already shown his value to the mission. A lot of times when we come in like this, there's friction between us and the townies—" She paused, remembering that Jake was a "townie."

But he laughed, and asked Quinn to continue.

"Clyde's been great at building teams between your men and my agents," Quinn said. She leaned forward. "Jake, he's got us working as one on the mission. If you're good with sharing Grace's identity with him, I'm in."

"Fine," Jake responded. He stood and shook Quinn's hand. "You run a tight ship, Quinn," he said.

She grinned, and looked human to Jake for the first time.

"And please," he said. "Call me Jake."

"I'm Ann, Jake," the agent said.

181

Jake opened the door and motioned to Clyde to come back inside.

"Have a seat, Clyde," he said. "What we're about to tell you has to stay in this room. I don't want you to even tell Tina or Esther. Can I have your word on that?"

"Of course, Jake. What is it?"

"You asked what Grace has to do with what's been going on. Well, she's a special agent working with the FBI. She's in charge of the mission here in the Bay to capture the terrorist we're trying to find, Major Vorack."

"Holy shit! Holy shit! I can't believe what you're telling me Jake."

"Hold on, Clyde, I couldn't either. Catch your breath. There's more."

"Grace is inside the Fisher Island facility right now," Agent Quinn said. "She's trying to find out what the Major's up to. He's planning something big this weekend. We don't know what yet. We suspect he's using Summerfair as a diversion."

Jake spoke from the heart when he said, "We've got to hope that the Russians haven't figured out that Grace is on our team. We don't have much time. How we move on this is still in Grace's hands, until we find out what the Major is about to do. She promised me she'd keep in contact, but I'm worried. We haven't heard from her."

"Agent Quinn," Clyde said, "What's your take on this?"

"Call me Ann, Clyde," Quinn responded. "Special Agent Grace Cooper is an excellent, capable, experienced agent. She's very smart. She's been in tough situations before. She will get in touch somehow." Her next words were aimed directly at Jake. "I'm not worried about her. She's good at what she does."

"You'd better be right."

I know, Quinn thought.

"Sheriff, we just can't sit still while we wait to hear from Grace," Clyde said. "Question: where do you think they've relocated the base after they burned down the house. Any thoughts on that?"

"What about Crook Neck Island?" Jake said. "There's an old abandoned lighthouse out there. They might be able to use that."

"How about taking one of Tinker's boats, dress like fishermen and check it out," suggested Clyde.

"Good idea, Clyde. Get Sam and Ben on it right away. Tell them we heard there was a report that someone was illegally living in the lighthouse, but we didn't want to confront them yet."

"We need to keep away from Fisher Island, but I'd like to post a lookout to keep an eye on it. How about someone with some high-powered binoculars up at the top of the Ridge after dark, when they usually signal movement back and forth. Who's available?"

"How about Turner?"

"Sounds good," Jake agreed. "Tell him we're watching for illegal fishing boats; make up something. He'll know soon enough. I'd like that list of men from Farmsville too. Thanks."

"Agent Quinn, Ann, what resources would the FBI have ready for action?"

"We have about fifty agents, a scuba team and two helicopters. Director Thompson could have them here in a few hours. He could have as many motorized pontoon boats as you need here."

"It sounds great. My only concern goes back to that mole in the FBI alerting Vorack that we're on to him. Any ideas, Ann?"

"I have a secure line to Director Thompson in case Agent Cooper isn't available. I'll talk it over with him."

"Fine. I'd like to be able to call a meeting with the rest of the team tomorrow afternoon at 2:00."

"Jake," asked Clyde. "I'll take over monitoring Summerfair for you, if you want to devote more time to working with the FBI and getting this creep before he gets away or blows up the Bay—or both."

"Thanks, Clyde. Sounds good. Put some extra people on the parade route."

"Anything else, Jake?" Clyde asked.

"Yeah, Clyde," Jake said, a hint of a smile on his face. "You forgot the coffee."

"Yeah," Ann laughed. "What's up with that?"

Forty-four

Later that day, Sam walked over to Jake, standing at the water cooler, and asked if he could speak privately in his office.

"Sure, what's up?" Jake asked after the two men were seated.

"You know how we came back from the Morefield House raid thinking somebody tipped them off?"

"Yeah?"

"Well, I've been watching one of Agent Quinn's men, Knox. He seems to use his phone a lot when the others don't. Usually, he steps outside the back of the building to make his calls. The calls are usually made after he's been talking with Agent Quinn. Maybe I'm being too suspicious, Jake, but this whole business has us all a little edgy."

"What do you mean?" Jake asked.

"Well, there are a lot of rumors flying around the

office. I heard one of the Feds say something about Russian terrorists and the Morefield House. We knew there was something not right up there, but Russian terrorists?"

"It's complicated," Jake said. Boy, was it, he thought. But Jake understood the danger of too much uncertainty. He and Quinn had to start sharing the bigger picture with the team. "We plan to call a meeting tomorrow to bring you all up to date. Be patient a little longer."

"OK, Jake, thanks for letting me blow off some steam," Sam said.

"No problem. And Sam—"

"Yeah?"

"Continue to watch Knox, especially after tomorrow's meeting here. And ask Chuck to come in would you?"

Jake got up as Chuck came in.

"Chuck, with all your electronic know-how, is it possible to tap into someone's private cell phone?"

"Possible? Yes. Legal? No."

"OK, here's what I'm going to ask you to do for me. And don't tell anyone. It has to be done before tomorrow, let's say about 1:00. Can you do it?"

"What've you got in mind, Chief?"

Forty-five

Friday morning at 5 a.m., a small boat moved slowly toward the mainland. It stayed as close to the rocky shore of the south end of Fisher Island as safety would allow, avoiding detection by the towering lighthouse above it. The early morning rainstorm had let up, but the sea was still dark and roiling. The lacey seafoam spray slid over the rail and down into the boat and curtained the hull. The skiff rocked back and forth on the roller coaster ride to the mainland.

Grace, wrapped tightly in her rain poncho, clung desperately to Dimitri's arm while cradling the waterproof box on her lap. It helped her to close her eyes and shut out the stinging spray. The thought of Jake was the only thing that made her happy.

The burly hulk, Boris, at the helm, seemed unmoved by the dangerous crossing and said nothing to the two of them huddled in the back. He

187

maneuvered the boat around the rocks, while small breakers battered its sides.

Yelling over the noise of the crashing surf, Boris focused the single beam of the running light toward where they'd pull in.

"Expect to get wet," he shouted.

Really, thought Grace, what a surprise!

She held tighter to the box as the boat struck a rock, bounced off, and grounded in the turbulent shallows.

Disembarking in the ankle-deep foam, the three figures bent forward wind whipped by frantic willow tree branches and made their way up a winding path. Grace could see the cabins over the next rise. No one was around that early, especially with the threatening weather. Ahead, their black Jeep Wrangler glistened in the rain, spotlighted in the beam of the overhead security lamp pole. She pulled at Boris' poncho and pointed toward cabin 18.

Boris just shook his head.

"Get in the car," he said.

Dimitri looked over at Grace and gave her a grim smile.

Boris checked his watch: 6 a.m. They'd better get going if they were to get to the reservoir by 10. Boris opened the trunk of the Jeep and threw in the Kalashnikov AK-107 rifle. He kept his pistol stuck in his waistband and a hunting knife strapped to his left ankle. As he slid behind the wheel, he took the pistol and placed it between his legs.

"Grace, in front; Dimitri, you ride in back."

Who died and made you commissar? Grace thought as Dimitri shrugged.

"You keep looking out window to be sure no one

is following us, yes? We should be there in about two hours. Enjoy the ride." He looked at them both and laughed.

As a light went on in a cabin at the end of the road, the Jeep made its way toward town down Exeter Street, carefully paralleling and avoiding Main Street. Everything was quiet. Grace looking down the side streets only saw the zippered tents sitting there waiting in anticipation of the Summerfair show opening in the morning. As they neared Beldon Street leading to the sheriff's station, they became aware of lights and a group of men standing outside. Boris pressed the gas pedal and sped ahead. Grace thought she noticed Jake's cruiser. Jake, she thought, wishing she had her phone. He had to be wondering why she hadn't called. She closed her eyes and inhaled deeply. Maybe she'd have that chance yet.

As the sun tried to peep through the thick clouds, the jeep left the paved road and started on the muddy trail to New Barnum Reservoir. The rutted road was still awash and covered with leaves and twigs. The car slid from side to side at times, almost ending up in the bushes that lined the roadbed. Boris swore in Russian most of the way.

Dimitri fingered the coiled steel wire in his coat pocket and wondered why Boris never searched them. Boris wasn't good at reasoning. He guessed he wanted the two of them to feel safe until the job was done and then he'd shoot them. He needed them. Boris didn't know how to release the spybird.

Dimitri waited. As they came over a small rise, the car headlights illuminated a wide deep puddle of water covering the road ahead. Dimitri knew Boris would have to slow down to navigate his way through it. Grace glanced back over her shoulder at Dimitri, who nodded. She was ready.

As Boris slowed, Dimitri reached over the seatback and deftly slipped the wire over Boris's head and around his neck. He was so skilled and quick that Boris didn't realize what was happening. His hands flew off the wheel. He frantically grabbed at his neck, causing the car to swerve sharply to the left. As his body arched, his foot pushed down on the accelerator. The car careened forward into the bushes and turned over on its side. Dimitri never let go.

"Grace, Grace, Are you OK?"

Dimitri could see her slumped forward, hanging limply by her seat belt.

He managed to slide his hand between the seats and grasp her shoulder.

He shook her again and she stirred. Her head came up and he could see a gash across her forehead, the blood trickling down into one eye.

"Grace, talk to me."

She groaned and opened her eyes. Everything looked blurry. "I hear you. Where are you? What happened?"

"Boris is dead and we're on our side in the Jeep. I need for you to try and open your door. I'm stuck back here. You have to get out and open the back door and pull me up. Can you do that?"

"I—I, don't know. I'll try."

"Try, we've got to get out of here."

Grace closed her eyes again.

"Grace!" Dimitri yelled.

She opened her eyes and tried to open her door. It

was like pushing an elephant. Every time she got it open, it would close again.

"OK, stop," Dimitri said. "I'll see if I can squeeze up and get my door open."

Grace closed her eyes again.

"Don't go to sleep, Grace. Keep your eyes open!"

Dimitri finally maneuvered himself to a kneeling position. He felt lucky he hadn't broken anything, but he ached all over. He used whatever strength he had left and finally found himself outside the car. With great effort, he dislodged Grace from her seat and carried her up the embankment at the side of the road. Going back to the trunk, he found their picnic chest. Opening it, he pulled out an unbroken bottle of vodka and some napkins. He poured some of the liquor on Grace's head.

"Ow, stop!" Grace's arm flew up and almost knocked the bottle out of Dimitri's hand.

"Open your eyes," Dimitri demanded. "Stop fighting me."

"Dimitri?"

"Do you think you can sit up?"

He put his arm around her shoulders and lifted her to an upright position.

"Ow."

"Here, take a drink of this, you'll feel better," he said as he offered her the half-empty vodka bottle. "Anything broken? Try and move your arms and legs."

She nodded and slowly did as she was told.

"OK?"

She nodded yes again.

"OK, just sit there. I'm going back down to see if I can find that cursed spybird box and see if I can try

191

to get Boris out of the car. I really don't want anyone to find him here."

Grace rolled over on her knees. Supporting herself on the crumpled car, she managed to stand up. "I'm feeling a little more awake. Can I help?" she said weakly, still holding the red stained piece of cloth napkin against her aching head.

"Wait. Don't move. I'm coming back. I don't want you to fall. Watch the mud."

Dimitri looked ahead toward the east. The sky was starting to brighten. At least they'd be able to see their way back. He wasn't sure if Grace could make it.

A few moments later, Dimitri emerged from some bushes twenty feet in front of the car.

"I was able to pull that pig Boris through the open window and stash him in the weeds," Dimitri said. "No one will find him for a while if they spot the car. I've got the box. Can you walk?"

Grace nodded yes.

"It's only 8:00. Vorack isn't expecting us back until 4:00 this afternoon. Maybe we have time to get back and cleaned up before they start looking for us. You need a proper bandage on that cut and we need another car. There's a lot to do."

All Grace could think about was how she was going to reach Jake. She had to tell him what's about to happen. If she could get back in town alone somehow or maybe get to a phone... She cursed herself for not telling Jake about the cabin. Quinn knew about the cabin. Maybe she'll look there for them, maybe. If they went back to the cabin, she'd try to sneak out and use the office phone. She'd find a way. She had to.

Forty-six

Jake looked at the clock on the wall across from his desk: 2:00.

He got up to see if everyone was at the station for the meeting. As he looked around the crowded room, he made eye contact with Chuck, who gave him a thumbs up. Good, Jake thought.

Agent Quinn sat at Sam's desk, her agents stood behind her. Jake began the meeting by going back to the Morefield House destruction and filled them in on the whole story as he knew it to date. He asked for questions, with both he and Agent Quinn answering what they could. At no time was Grace brought into the conversation.

Jake told the teams to meet at the high school gymnasium the next night at 8:30. At that time, they'd be briefed.

"This is privileged information, fellas," Jake said as the meeting ended. "Agent Quinn has already explained this to her agents, but let me repeat her words. This information is not to go beyond the station. Don't tell you wives, your sweethearts, and if you talk in your sleep, sleep here!"

At that everyone laughed. The teams broke up into small groups going over what they'd heard. Jake stood outside his office, observing their movement. He motioned to Chuck to go into his office. Chuck went in and closed the door. Jake sat on the edge of Ben's desk, talking to him, but watching the agents as they moved around the room. He saw Knox say something to Agent Quinn and head toward the back door.

Jake excused himself and went into his office where Chuck sat wearing a pair of earphones. Without saying a word, Chuck nodded to Jake to come over and handed him the headset.

Jake heard a man's voice saying something in what sounded like Russian. Jake grabbed a pencil and quickly wrote a note to Chuck. *Are you recording this?*

Chuck nodded yes. Before the conversation ended, the man said in English, "Pleasure doing business with you. Happy to be of service." And then he said something in Russian that Jake couldn't understand.

Jake immediately took off the earphones and opened the office door. He looked toward the back of the room just as Knox returned.

Jake closed the door once more and smiled at Chuck.

"Thanks Chuck, looks like we landed a big catfish."

"Bottom-feedin' mole," Chuck said.

"Leave the tape here. Please, do not say a word to anyone about this."

"You don't have to worry about that, my friend."

Jake stuck his head out of his office, and called to Agent Quinn.

Forty-seven

"Get in," Dimitri said to Grace, opening the door of the truck.

He had hotwired a Ford pickup he found nearby behind an empty house, and returned to get Grace, whom he had left hiding out behind an abandoned produce stand near the Barnum Reservoir cutoff.

Grace climbed in, laid her head back on the seat rest, and closed her eyes. The cut on her head throbbed.

"Grace, there's got to be a phone in the gas station we passed this morning. It's about a mile from here. I've got the phone number of this guy I know, someone I used to work with. He'll get us out of here and up to Canada."

He looked over at her. "You OK?"

"Yeah."

"I think we'll head back to the cabin afterward, unless you have a better idea."

Grace opened her eyes. "Do you think we should go back to the cabin? That's the first place they'll check once Vorack doesn't hear from Boris."

"Yeah, I know. We'll be out of there before the good old Major starts to get worried. Wait until I make the call," he answered as they pulled into the station. "You stay here. I don't want anyone to see how bad you look. I look bad enough. They'd get suspicious."

After Dimitri went inside the station, Grace saw a man in overalls head out toward the back of the truck. She watched him in the side mirror as he started to fill the tank. She pulled open the glove compartment, trying to find a pencil, anything to write with. She already had a scrap of old newspaper in her hand. She could give him Jake's number. At least they'd know she was still alive.

She was about to roll down the window to speak to him and saw Dimitri coming out of the station. Dimitri paid him and got back into the truck.

Grace let her head fall back on the headrest again and crumpled up the paper. She moved her arm through the open window as they pulled out. Entering the highway, she opened her hand and the tiny piece of paper disappeared. She berated herself for not talking to the man right away.

"Well, good news," Dimitri said. "I got ahold of him. He's going to help us. If we could manage to stay put for the night, he'd have everything arranged for us to slip over the border by noon tomorrow. It should take about four hours to get to where we're to meet him."

"How're our supplies?" Grace asked.

"I picked up Boris' gun and there are two more

stashed in the cabin," Dimitri said. "Besides, there's food there and medical supplies. You need to clean up that wound on your forehead. Now lay back and try to relax."

Relax? thought Grace. You're out of your mind. Besides, she wasn't sure about going back to the cabin.

In his office on Fisher Island, the Major kept looking at the clock. Boris was two hours overdue. Not to worry, he told himself. He could always count on Boris. All would be fine, he thought. He'd be back soon. He was anxious to get a report about the launching of the spybird. He trusted Boris. He knew his mission had to be successful and smiled thinking of Saturday's results and Sunday's confirming headlines. Yes. It probably just took Boris longer than expected to get rid of the bodies. Well, maybe he should send Karl over. If something went wrong, Boris might go to the cabin.

Dimitri had yielded to Grace's concerns and agreed to stay away from the cabin. Instead, he parked the truck on a rise behind some trees. They then piled shrubbery around it. From their hidden spot, they could view the cabin and surrounding area. Grace yearned for the soft beds and shower in the cabin, but felt safer bedded down in the cramped confines of the truck.

About 10 p.m., she heard a sound.

"Dimitri," she whispered. She pointed toward the cabin. They heard footsteps. Someone tried the locked door. A ray from a flashlight danced across the windows and then went out.

I was right, Grace thought. They heard the front door being opened. Whoever it was had a pass key.

After a few endless moments, they saw a dark figure go down the stairs. Dimitri left the truck and slipped down to level ground. He moved back toward the cabin and looked around the side of the building. A man was crossing the parking lot below heading toward the owner's cabin. He saw the figure, illuminated by the porch light, talking to the owner and pointing toward their cabin. The owner shook his head. The man got into his car and left. Out of the darkness, Dimitri heard Grace's voice. "Did you recognize him?"

"Not sure. It was too dark. We need to leave here in the morning. I want to be out of here by 5 a.m.. They'll be back."

Forty-eight

At sun up on Saturday, Main Street started to fill with Summerfair tourists. Jake's deputies had cleared the wide street of cars the night before. Tents lined the sidewalk and spilled out into Overlook Park on the beach side of the street. Some people had arrived early to get a good view of the festivities. They sat in lawn chairs along both sides of the parade route drinking coffee and reading the morning paper.

At 8:00, Mayor Wilkes climbed onto the red, white and blue bunting draped podium below the statue of old General Litchfield and addressed the expectant crowd.

A six-year-old girl held tightly to her father's hand and tried to look interested. She could only think of the parade and the promised visit to the circus in the afternoon. She'd been going to the circus since she was four. She'd hold her mommy's hand watching the tents go up. Giant posts were hammered into the ground. Tall poles with thick ropes attached laid next to them. Trained elephants would pull on the ropes and the gigantic tent with flags flying atop the poles would pop up out of nowhere. What a surprise! She'd always clap her hands.

She looked up beyond the towering people surrounding her and saw the sky fill with balloons. It was better than her birthday! She could hear band music coming from somewhere. Her father pulled her by the hand and they disappeared into the moving crowd.

The parade was starting to line up at the far end of Litchfield Park. Mayor Wilkes adjusted his sash across his shoulder and then got into a white Cadillac convertible on loan from Harvard Autos. The standard bearers and the Ladies of Hibernia holding the Caswell Bay banner looked back for the mayor's signal to begin.

Forty-nine

Dimitri woke up with a start. "Damn," he said out loud. He peered out of the truck window at a car sitting over in the parking lot near the cabins. He knew it didn't belong to anyone staying in the park. He surmised it could be someone stationed there to watch for Boris. It might even be the FBI on their trail, waiting to see what move they'd make next. He looked at his watch: 7a.m..

"Damn, damn, damn."

They had to get out of there. He looked over at Grace, slumped in the passenger seat. Her bloody bandage had come askew, but it appeared that her head wound had closed. He nudged her.

Grace opened her eyes. "What is it?"

"Get up, hurry. The cabin's being watched. Driving out of here is no longer an option. We're going to have to try to get out through the back and hope no one's out there watching."

Dimitri opened the carefully wrapped box and took out the cylinder containing Vorack's precious spybird. Opening the top of the mechanism, he removed the capsule of toxin. He wrapped it in some foil and pushed it into the seat between the backrest and bottom cushions.

"Dimitri, what are you doing?"

"You leave first. If we get split up, I'll meet you behind the Greyston Farm. After you leave, I'm going to release the spybird and send it past where the car is parked. Maybe they'll follow it and not us. Let's go."

He opened his door; she did the same. Both of them slipped out and down to the ground behind the cabin. Dimitri took out his pistol and motioned it toward the hill trail to his right.

"Go, I'll cover you."

He watched Grace run up the hill, waited until she was out of sight and then moved to the side of the cabin facing away from the car. Still hidden from view, Dimitri reached around the corner of the building and released the spybird. He glanced over and saw two men get out of the car. A bald, heavyset man focused his binoculars on the bird's path. The other man in the red cap looked back at the cabin, turned and said something to the other man. Red cap started heading in Dimitri's direction.

Shit! Running as fast as he could up the hill and into the forest, Dimitri started down the path toward town. He wanted to increase the distance between the two of them. He kept looking over his shoulder, almost smacking into a tree. Not seeing anyone behind him, he thought the red cap man might have spotted Grace and followed her instead. A moment later, he saw the red cap not fifty feet behind him.

"Stop!" the man yelled.

Dimitri rounded a bend in the path and ran off to the side and hid under a rock outcropping. Crouching low, he peered around the corner. The man had stopped with his back to him. He had his cap off now and was mopping his brow with a handkerchief. Dimitri silently took out a pistol strapped to his leg and moved out of hiding. He stood up ready to fire, when he heard a familiar voice above and behind him.

"Don't move, Dimitri. The Major won't be happy to hear we found you alive. I can guess what has happened to our good friend, Boris. The Major really liked Boris—Boris, so reliable, but apparently, Boris, so stupid. Now drop the gun and turn around slowly."

Dimitri dropped his arm to his side, but didn't let go of the gun.

He looked up and saw the Major's bodyguard, Karl staring down at him from atop the rock outcropping. He should have recognized that bald head back at the cabin, even from a distance. Dimitri's hand automatically raised again. He heard a shot and looked up, waiting to see Karl topple from above—but he didn't. He looked down and watched a bright red stain start to spread over his own chest. Dropping to his knees, his last view was of a red cap waving at him.

"The Major says, bye-bye."

Grace heard a gunshot behind her. She stopped dead in her tracks. She listened and heard nothing more. Slowly, she doubled back up the path seeking shelter from sight as she did. She hadn't gone far when she caught a glimpse of two men busily occupied with something on the ground. She stopped.

Moving off the path and to her left, she tried not to step on anything that would reveal her presence. She hid out of sight and decided to stay put. A few moments later, she heard them coming down the path and moved deeper into hiding as they passed by. Catching the last view of the back of one of the men, she noticed he wore a red cap. She didn't see the other man in front of him. She didn't move from her position for close to a half hour.

When she was sure they weren't coming back, she once again started her ascent. She looked for anything out of place. She sat down on a rock close to where she'd first seen the men. She scanned the area again. Her eyes noticed something shiny, partially obscured by some leaves. When she picked it up, she fell back onto the rock, her legs suddenly unable to hold her up. She turned it over and over in the palm of her hand. It was a coin… a lion's head on one side and a hawk on the other. She had seen Dimitri turn it over and over in his hand when he was thinking deeply about something.

She bent down where she'd found the coin and brushed the leaves aside. Part of Dimitri's jacket became visible. She could see blood stains and she realized who the shot was meant for.

She looked quickly up and down the path listening for signs she wasn't alone. She jumped hearing the sound of twigs snapping to her right— only a squirrel. A wave of fear swept over her. If they could find Dimitri so quickly, how long would it be before they found her? The Major wouldn't rest until he she was dealt with. She had to find Jake. Maybe, if she were lucky, just maybe, they could capture Vorack before he escaped with his doomsday device.

When she reached town, she stopped and stood at the top of the last rise of the hill before it dropped down behind the library. From there, she could see a large segment of Main Street. The opening day parade filled the street below, the crowds lining the route, roaring with excitement. It must have just started, she thought.

Looking to the right, she saw the mayor sitting in a white Cadillac convertible waving to the welcoming crowd. He grinned as if it were the best day of his life—It certainly wasn't hers.

Moving slowly behind the mayor's car, she saw the Summerfair King and Queen happily acknowledging the whistles and cheers of the crowd. Tina had told her the Queen's pink satin evening gown was the same one the girl's mother had worn when she was Summerfair Queen twenty years ago. A bouquet of red roses lay across her lap. They both looked so excited and so young, Grace thought.

The Garden Club float followed. They'd created a huge yellow honey bee hovering over an enormous deep red chrysanthemum. Everything was made out of daisies, roses and dyed carnations. It was amazing and it seemed unreal after all she'd just been through. The loud brassy sound of the high school band moving into view on her left brought her back to reality. They were playing their school fight song, as the cheerleaders threw their batons high in the air.

She started down toward Main Street, knowing the hitmen were waiting for her, but where? Vendors were everywhere hawking their wares through the crowd. She hoped the frantic activity would help to prevent her discovery. She made it to the curb just as the circus performers began strutting by. A seven-foot clown with red bushy hair grabbed Grace and started to dance with her. She kept trying to pull away and kept telling him, no. When he finally released her, she was on the opposite side of the road. She almost fell over a little girl with an orange balloon who was jumping up and down with excitement. Grace turned around and side-stepped a passing elephant.

"Look out, lady!" the trainer called down to her. "Stay out of the road!"

Grace squeezed in between some chairs and moved inside a tent selling sports clothes and souvenirs. She bought a visor cap with a sailboat embroidered on the bill. She tucked her hair under the cap and bought a pair of dark sunglasses as well.

Peering out from the safety of the tent, she could see a contingent of the Veterans of Foreign Wars waving small American flags passing by. It wouldn't be long before the parade ended. She could hear the clang of the fire engine bell in the distance. She still had to cross back over the street to the Sheriff's Department.

She moved slowly down the sidewalk, trying to appear invisible. She kept bumping into people. A little girl brushed her ice cream cone against her jacket arm. The girl's mother was apologetic. Grace just smiled and moved on. Don't attract attention, she thought.

Seeing Seaside Avenue, she thought, just two more blocks. Up ahead, across the street, she spotted two men standing high on the top of the front steps of the bank building, looking the crowd over. One wore a red cap. It had to be them.

Suddenly the second man turned toward her.

"Karl! Oh, God," she said under her breath, "not Karl."

She ducked behind one of the tents facing the two men. Just as she turned, a portly man carrying his son on his shoulders bumped into her, knocking her hat to the ground. Grace's blonde hair tumbled free over her shoulders, shining like spun gold. Both men looked in her direction. Karl pointed.

Grace took off, heading back in the direction of the 4- Poster, cutting in between two passing floats. One of the costumed girls atop the Tinker's Hardware float recognized her.

"Grace, Grace, up here." She called out to her, waving frantically, trying to get her attention and threw a piece of candy in her direction.

Sheesh, Grace thought, do you want to just paint a target on my back? She jumped in between two people sitting on the curb, accidentally knocking the bag of popcorn out of the lady's hand. The husband got up and called after Grace. Grace yelled back, "Sorry, sorry."

Fifty

"Sheriff, I just received a call from the owner of the Bide a Wee cabins," Turner said, poking his head into Jake's office. "He said he heard a gunshot about an hour ago. He apologized for not calling it in sooner. He said he was coming out of his office and saw two men he didn't recognize as renters. One of the men had binoculars. Figured he was a bird watcher."

"Tell me more, Turner," Jake said.

"He tried to see what the man was looking at and thought he saw a small mechanical plane. He thought it was a kid's toy. At any rate the two of them took off running up the hill behind one of the cabins. Didn't see what they were after. About fifteen minutes later, he heard a gunshot. He's a hunter and said that's how he knew what he heard was a shot. He didn't go to investigate. Thought he'd let you do that."

Jake didn't believe in coincidences. This could be a lead in tracking down Grace. "Good work, Turner." The young deputy beamed. "Take Chuck and go up and check it out. Call me as soon as you find out anything, OK?"

Turner almost bumped into Tina as he turned to leave. She brushed past him, only stopping when she reached Jake's desk.

"Chief, Chief—"

"Whoa, slow down, Tina. What's up?"

"Ben just called in. He thought he spotted Grace in town. It looked as if two men were chasing her. He's got them in his sight and wants to know what to do."

Jake leaped up from his desk. "Tell him to follow them, but don't use force unless absolutely necessary and no gunfire," he said. "Be careful, lots of families with small kids. Tina, tell Ben to call me with her whereabouts. I need to know where they are at all times. We're on our way."

Jake stopped to open his desk drawer and change guns. He didn't want to attract any more attention than had already happened and quickly screwed on a silencer. He hoped he wouldn't need it.

"Tina, go tell Agent Quinn what's happening. I'll call her with an update. Hurry. I'm going to get started."

"Clyde, Sam, come with me."

Grace saw the 4-Poster Inn ahead. Running up the front stairs, she startled Marge and her two nieces in the porch swing.

"Grace," Marge started to call out to her. The screen door slammed shut before she could finish her sentence. "Well, I'll be," Marge said to her nieces and started to follow Grace inside.

Looking through the lace covered front window, Grace saw the man in the red cap stop and look around. About ten yards behind him, she thought she saw Ben in the crowd. If she could signal to him, he might be able to help. She looked around the room for something she could use as a weapon and thought about the greenhouse.

She heard the front screen door slam, so she took off running through the lily garden and out the back through the white picket fence gate. Turning right, she started to head back toward Pickett's Point to the stand of trees where she knew the boat would be tied up. Maybe she could take it into the— she stopped.

Down the hill, blocking her path was the red cap man. He was kneeling now, looking up the hill at her, in a shooter's stance. Instinctively, she dropped to the ground. Just as she did, she glanced up and saw Ben come up behind the man and hit him over the head with the butt of his revolver. A father with his little son, who was holding a blue balloon, were coming up the path behind Ben. The man picked up the squealing little boy and ran back down the path.

Grace started to get up and turn and run. Suddenly, she saw Karl smiling at her just outside the garden gate. She could see the gun this time, the sun glinting off the barrel. There was no place for her to go and she stood like a statue. But as he came toward her, he suddenly fell to his knees and then pitched forward to land face down in the pathway.

Grace still didn't move, not comprehending what she'd seen. Jake stepped into the sunlight removing the silencer from his pistol. He looked over at Grace and smiled.

211

She felt her body going limp, her lungs releasing her pent up breath. Relief swept over her.

"Oh, my God, it's you!" was all she could say.

Jake ran toward her. "Are you all right?"

She threw her arms around him, hugging him tightly, her tears dampening his shirt collar. "You're like an angel from heaven. I thought it was all over."

Freeing herself from their embrace, Grace pulled herself together. "Listen, Jake. We've got to move fast. I know everything. Let's get back to the station where we can talk. Don't worry, I'm fine. I'm not hurt. Quick, let's go," she said grabbing his arm.

Then she spotted Quinn arriving with her agents.

"Wait, wait, there's Ann," Grace said. "I've got to talk to her."

Before he could say anything, Grace ran over to Quinn. After they hugged, Jake heard her say to Grace, "You're like a cat with nine lives. Thank God you're all right."

He noticed Knox wasn't with her.

"Listen up everyone," Jake said trying to get their attention. "It's getting a little crowded up here right now. I don't want any tourists joining us. Ben, head to the station and bring a squad car around to Exeter Street. When you get back here, you and Clyde take our cuffed guest back to the lockup. We also need to get the coroner and his crew here to say a prayer over our belated friend. Clyde, call him and tell him to come here the same way. We want to avoid Main Street at all cost."

He turned to Agent Quinn. "I guess you'll call Director Thompson and let him know Grace is OK, but we're still moving ahead with our plan, right?"

"He's already here, Jake," Quinn said, "flew by

helicopter from Portland a half hour ago."

"So, you've talked with him, Ann?"

"Oh yes. Everything's been straightened out. Is that what you wanted to know?"

Grace looked puzzled. "What's going on?"

"I think what Ann is trying to tell us is that Agent Knox has been arrested. He's our FBI mole who's been putting you and the mission in danger."

"That's unbelievable. You sure? How did you know?"

"It's a long story. We need to hear yours first. Let's get going. Coming Ann?"

"You bet." She looked at Jake and smiled. Well what do you know? He thought, a real smile.

Fifty-one

Just before they left the back yard of the 4-Poster, Clyde came over to Jake and handed him his cell phone.

"Here, Jake. It's Chuck. They found a body up on the trail."

"Chuck, talk to me."

"Listen, we found a body up here on the Wilson Trail behind the cabins. Looks like a professional hit… one shot through the heart. Looks as if it came from behind him. The body's been buried. We only uncovered the upper torso. Didn't want to disturb the crime scene any further. The rest was left for the forensic team. Not too far from the body, Turner found a pistol, not fired recently. I called in the description. Turned out to be a Russian issue, Makarov PM pistol. After the body gets back to the coroner and processed, I'll send his photo and prints through the system and see if we can get a match."

"Russian, I'm not surprised. Look, tell Turner he should stay with the body and I'll get the coroner

214

and an investigative team up there as soon as they finish here. I'm sending Sam up there to head it up."

"Clyde, let's get going. I want to learn more about Mr. Red Cap."

"Grace, how're you holding up? How did you hurt your head?" Jake asked, tenderly touching her forehead.

"I'll be OK, Jake. It's a long story. I've gotten over the initial shock that I was about to be killed. Thank God you got there when you did. I had no way to contact you. Vorack took my phone, and my weapon."

"I'm just glad you're safe. Look, Grace, we just got a call from Chuck. Apparently shots were fired up by the cabins this morning. He and Turner found a body up on the old Wilson Trail. Do you know anything about this?"

"Yeah Jake. I know the man who was killed up on Wilson Trail. He was the Russian agent I was working with. We were being chased by these two," she said looking back over her shoulder at the red cap man and the dead man lying outside the garden gate. "The dead man on the trail is Dimitri Povash. He's the one I told you about earlier. These two men are Vorack's henchmen. The one you shot dead went by the name of Karl. I never knew his last name. If you fingerprint these two men, Director Thompson can check with Interpol and give us more info. I'll tell you the whole story on the way to the station. I know Vorack's plan. We don't have any time. Now, please, let's get going."

"OK, OK." He took Grace by the hand. "You're coming with me. I'm not letting you out of my sight from now on. Got it?"

Grace just smiled at him. "No problem, Sheriff."

Back at the department, Jake headed into his office with Quinn and Grace. After the door closed, Grace filled everyone in about Vorack's plans as she knew them. She was happy that Jake and Ann had already taken the initiative to set up the raid that night. They were all as ready as they were going to be. The FBI would furnish the big guns. Grace was mentally and emotionally ready, geared up for the night ahead of her. It was good to be alive. She and Jake just had to survive the night.

"A lot to do before tonight. Ann, would you mind leaving us alone?"

After Quinn left the room, Jake closed the blinds. He took Grace in his arms. They held each other for a long time, neither one wanting the moment to end.

When Jake finally reopened the office door, he called over to Clyde. "C'mon, Clyde, We're going back to the lockup and take a look our red cap guy."

"What's this perp's name? Do we have a file on him yet?"

"Don't know yet. We sent the prints over to Director Thompson a few minutes ago. We're waiting for a reply."

When they went to the cell, all the perp would say was, "I tell you nothing. Get me lawyer. I know United States law."

On the way back to his office, Tina motioned for Jake to come over to her desk. The station was now filling up with FBI agents, mingling with his own deputies.

"The Interpol report just came in, Jake. He's Russian. Russian mafia, here? Hard to believe."

"What about the dead man?"

"The other perp you whacked is an interesting character. The body will be on the way to the morgue for autopsy in about half an hour. His prints were taken and sent out also. You'll be surprised when you hear who he is."

"Let me take a look at that report."

"Yeah, they're both not nice boys, Jake. Apparently wanted assassins working for the Russian Mafia," Tina said. "How about that! And the one in the woods is that Dimitri Povash you've been looking for. He was wanted in Bulgaria and Turkey as well. The one you popped was identified as Karl Novia, on the FBI's most wanted list of foreign assassins no less. His file was sealed though. Interesting. Why would big name guys like that be doing in Caswell Bay? Looks like Vorack's not taking any chances."

Grace was seated at Turner's desk looking through a report she'd just received from Director Thompson. She called over to Chuck. "Bring our new friend into the interrogation room. Check his restraints, both wrist and ankles. I don't want him getting away. Where's Agent Quinn?"

"She's over at the gym organizing tonight's meeting."

Grace closed the FBI folder she'd been reading, stood up and walked over to Jake. "Come on, Jake," "Now we know a little more about him, let's go back and see what we can get out of him now."

The sullen man was slumped in his chair. He looked up as Jake and Grace came in and stood facing him.

"Hello, Gregor. I'm Special Agent Cooper of the FBI and this is Sheriff Mason. I know you're surprised to see me again, alive that is."

Gregor's looked up at Grace, in shock. FBI! Shit! he thought, but quickly regained his composure as Jake sat down across from him.

"I'm just a tourist here in America. I wanted to come here to see your lovely country. Maybe I become American too. What you think?"

"You're not an American, Gregor," Grace shot back. "You're just a nasty little assassin. That's what it says right here," as she waved the manila folder in front of his face. "I know a lot of people who would like to get their hands on you. How about your good old buddy, Igor Marstov? Should I give him a call? Or are you going to cooperate with us?"

The name struck a chord with the recalcitrant Russian. His demeanor changed instantly. "Well, what you want to know? See how cooperative I am being even without a lawyer."

He smiled broadly, letting a glint of light flash off of his two gold front teeth.

"OK, here's what you can do for us," Grace said. "I know your boss, Major Anton Vorack is anxious to hear from you. We have your cell phone. I want you to call your boss and tell him your mission here was perfect. You and Karl found Grace Cooper and Dimitri Povash, who admitted killing Boris. Then you and Karl killed the two of them. Tell him you and your friend will head back to the island after dark tonight. I also want you to tell the Major that they never got to the resevoir."

"What resevoir?"

"Just tell him that."

His smile now gone. Gregor asked, "Who told you about the island and all these people?"

Grace leaned in low over Gregor's shoulder. "I know a lot more than you think. I know about Vorack's nasty little plot."

"OK then, give me phone."

When the Major hung up, he was delighted. Well, at last, a turn for the better. Now we do have time, he thought. He sat back in his chair and poured himself a tall vodka and drank it down without taking a breath. He strolled into the monitoring center and scanned the screens. He took special interest in his pet scientist. Petrenko was where he should be. Vorack laughed to himself. A few more hours, little man, he said.

Petrenko sat bent over his lab work table. He looked at the small clock above him, embedded in the wall—2 p.m. Almost time for his coffee break, he thought.

Ilya entered the lab and stood with his back to the security camera, causing Petrenko to swing around and face his security guard friend.

"llya, is everything all right?"

"We need to talk, my friend. Go back to your work and listen before Valeria comes back in here. I'm going to tell you something you were not to know, but I have come to care about you. You have helped me, what do you say, find myself. You're a good man."

"What is it?"

"Petrov told me the Major and everyone are leaving island tonight and—"

"What? Tonight you say?"

"You are in danger. Major Vorack is going to

eliminate the communication techs and you and your comrades as well. I want to help you, my friend, and ask a favor, a big favor."

Petrenko willed himself to not look up at the security camera. He nodded yes.

Suddenly Valeria opened the door, almost knocking Ilya down and stopped him in midsentence.

"Oh, sorry, Ilya, I didn't expect anyone so near the door. What are you doing here anyway?"

"I just had a message from the Major."

His eyes meet Petrenko's. He nodded toward the hallway.

Petrenko waited ten minutes and entered the safety of the restroom. He guessed Grace wasn't the only one to know about it. Sure enough, Ilya was waiting for him. "Ilya, talk fast."

"You have to escape. I will help you, but you must take me with you. I want to stay here in America and become teacher. Tonight, I'll get myself assigned to you and bring a disguise so you look like one of the workers. I know where there's a boat tied up at the end of the island and we can go to shore. We can make a new life. You must take me with you."

Petrenko thought that Grace hadn't given him a better plan.

"All right, what time?"

"I don't know yet, just be ready."

Fifty-two

By 9 p.m., the gymnasium was filled wall to wall with police and FBI agents. Tables holding weapons and ammunition at the front and protective gear on tables in the rear lined the gym. Catering trucks used to bring in the men and equipment undetected were still parked in back of the gym. Only the rear entrances were used. Even the security lights had been turned off.

The FBI had done an amazing job assembling so much so quickly. Half the motorized pontoon boats were already tied up at the south end of Pickett's Point. The other half, due to arrive by midnight would be based in a boat house on the north side of the marina. The helicopters were prepared to leave on a moment's notice.

"Everyone, please find a place to sit, the floor is a great place. Quiet please," shouted a tall black man with glasses and a bow tie. "My name is Blake Thompson, FBI Director. To my left is Special Agent Ann Quinn and Special Agent Grace Cooper, who will give you the details of tonight's assignment. To my right is Sheriff Jake Mason, who will be in charge of the assault. I commend all of you for your bravery in participating in this dangerous mission. The inexperienced among us

221

will be paired with someone who has seen this type of duty before. They will guide you through it. Special Agent Cooper will now fill you in."

"In three and a half hours we'll leave this place," Grace began. "Each of you has been assigned to a squad and has a leader. The assignment sheet is posted by the entrance if you haven't as yet found your squad. Your squad leader will be sure you have the weapons and protective gear you need and will give you your individual assignments. We want to complete the mission as quickly and efficiently as possible with as few casualties as possible." She turned and nodded her head at Jake.

"Sheriff Mason, will you continue, please."

"Our target tonight is Fisher Island and the capture of a Major Anton Vorack who has, as you know by now, set up a base below the surface of the glacial terrain. If you'll look to your right at the far wall, please."

A large projection screen lit up on the north wall of the gym showing a map of Caswell Bay and the adjacent island, Fisher Island.

"Without going into all the details, about fifty well-armed and prepared Russian terrorists occupy the facility. A Major Vorack is in command. Surprise will be our ally. As far as we know, the Major has not been informed of our plans. We've opted not to evacuate the town for two reasons. One, such an event would alert the target. The mayor, however, is prepared to sound the warning sirens if he's alerted to do so. The attack will surely awaken the town. That's unavoidable. The National Guard is on standby. But we hope to confine the attack to the island, thus avoiding injury to civilians. In the event that things go bad, we also have our own medical teams in place. Other neighboring towns will be contacted to supply medical help if needed."

The men and women began looking around the room. Everyone had the same thought—who'll be walking back and who'll be carried back after the raid?

"The Russians plan to depart the island tonight," Jake continued. "We have three objectives: find and isolate the boxes of weapons they've created; capture and detain the force on the island and all attached personnel; and catch Major Vorack. We want him alive if at all possible. This is a tall order. While we outnumber them, I am sure they have their defense system in place, especially tonight."

Agent Quinn stood up. "Hopefully, your squad leader can answer any further questions you may have," she said. "I want everyone to be in their final positions by 1:45 a.m. We'll move out at 2:30. Everyone, check your watches. It is now exactly 11:04. Be safe," and handed the microphone back to the Director.

"Before you leave here tonight," he began, "I want to tell you how much the country appreciates the heroism and courage of you brave men and women sitting in front of me. The leadership of the two Special Agents seated up here has been outstanding. On behalf of the President of the United States, please accept a nation's thanks for what you've done and what I'm sure you'll accomplish tonight. Again, thank you all and God be with you."

Fifty-three

By 1 a.m., most of the lights in the homes and hotels were turned off. A dog barked somewhere up near the point. In the bay, the water moved more rapidly toward shore and small white caps started to form.

A dim white light flashed on and off at the far end of Fisher Island; on and off, on and off. And then all was darkness. Even the security lights in the marina were dark.

By 2 a.m., no one heard the low muffled sound of the *Levongrad's* engine as it made anchorage near Fisher Island.

At the docking area hidden inside the island, workers in black hooded jumpsuits swarmed like ants, carrying boxes from their storage areas to the incoming boats. It was 2:20. The freighter had docked fifteen minutes ago. Two boatloads of the carefully packaged boxes containing Vorack's precious spybirds were already on their way to the *Levongrad*. The ship lay anchored in the Bay a quarter-mile west of the island.

From his vantage point twelve feet above the dock adjacent to the catwalk, Vorack watched the workers running quickly with sealed boxes, loading them onto the waiting boats.

"Over there, Kershav," Vorack barked into a bullhorn at one of the workers carrying a large waterproof box. "Over there— to the boat, you idiot."

He left the booth and went down into the melee. There couldn't be any mistakes, not now.

An hour ago, chemicals had been sprayed on the algae nearest the opening, to dissolve it. But the backwash created by the docking and leaving of the transport boats pushed more of the engine-clogging scum back toward the cave opening. Vorack ordered more spray immediately. He yelled at Petrov to get some men out there with poles. He couldn't let a little thing like algae foil their departure.

In the labs, deep within the island, technicians were packing the computers. The Major had told them to leave everything else behind, no exceptions. The storage room doors on the sub level stood open. The shelves of cylinders that once delighted the Major, stood empty. The huge toxin tank in Room 12, had been fully drained; its contents stored in large sealed vials three hours earlier by men in hazard suits.

The Major now stood on the loading dock, hovering over the crates containing the toxin like a mother hen. Nothing, he thought, could happen to these. They would never pay him if the toxin didn't show up as well. Since the test was not accomplished, he'd contacted the buyers and told them they would have the cylinders and their precious toxin in their hands within the week. They could perform their own test. He told them he'd return the money if they weren't satisfied. Of course, he had no intention of doing that.

Vorack was uneasy, however. Some key players were missing. "Has anyone seen Karl or Gregor? Petrov, go see if you can find them. I have to go back to my office. Bring Dr. Petrenko too."

Just then one of the workers bumped into Vorack knocking him into one of the crates.

Enraged, without hesitation, Vorack turned quickly, pulled out his revolver and shot the frightened worker. The box he was carrying crashing onto the dock. Everyone stopped in their tracks.

"Get back to work," he snapped. Pick up that box, get him out of here, throw him into the sea, the clumsy bastard. Now!" Still angry, he marched toward his office. "Finish loading the boats. I want to be out of here in one half hour. Whoever is not done and ready to go at that time will be left behind. Hurry up!"

Pushing his way through the bustling workers,back down the corridor to his office, he saw Valeria waving at him, trying to get his attention.

"Major, I was able to reach—"

Vorack grabbed her by the arm and shoved her through his office door.

"Don't ever give me personal messages in front of the crew, you hear me. Now where is the sub?"

"I'm sorry Major, I was just—"

"Now what is it?"

"The sub, Major. It is close. Major Blucor said he will pick you up off the north shore of Crook Neck Island at 0320. He wanted to know if you'll have the scientists with you."

"Tell him no. That's been taken care of."

"He'll watch for your signal as you approach. He said to be on time. He'll only wait twenty minutes for you."

Damn, the Major thought. I'd wanted the rendezvous earlier. I'll be out there like a sitting duck. I'll have to find a place near the shore.

He looked up as a shadow darkened the doorway. "Petrov, did you find them?"

"No Major. I looked for Dr. Petrenko, but no one has seen him either."

No, he thought to himself. Could Karl and Gregor have been captured? If they were here, they would've come directly to him by now. Now his anxiety level matched his anger. "We've got to move out of here fast. Petrov, find three men and tell them I said to search every inch of this island and don't come back until they can bring this scientist, this Dr. Petrenko with them."

Ten minutes later, the Major took two stairs at a time on his way back down to the dock. He needed to finish the loading and get his crates. He wasn't leaving without them. Just then he spotted Petrov headed his way, alone.

In the confusion of the shooting on the dock, two men, out of Vorack's range of vision, quickly walked toward the cave entrance. They were dressed like the others, but didn't carry any boxes.

Stechkin APS Rifles were slung over their shoulders. They continued onto the catwalk that lead them outside and onto the rocks surrounding the opening to the cave. Several men were bent down pulling algae away from the opening with long poles.

"Hey, you two, over here," one of the men with poles called to them. "We need more help."

A reply, in Russian, came from one of the two men. The man with the pole laughed. The two waved and continued moving on, stopping at the top of the ridge. From there, they had a view of the freighter and the boats coming and going to the ship. To the west, they saw the lights of Crook Neck Island in the distance. Hearing the sound of rocks tumbling down the hill in front of them, they instinctively crouched down. The noise stopped.

Moving slowly ahead once more, their way was suddenly blocked by a man dressed as they were, with a rifle in his hand— pointed directly at them. Again, softly spoken Russian flowed between the three men and the rifle was lowered. They spoke a little longer. The man with the rifle went back into hiding, concealed in darkness, hidden in the rocks. The other two continued slowly, heading toward the far end of the island. Every now and then, another encounter and more short conversations in Russian. Before they started downhill toward the sea, Ilya looked at Yuri Petrenko and pointed at the boat tied up below.

"Wait." Ilya stopped and listened. Another worker on guard? No, this was different. "Get down."

They both crouched low and then lay flat on the

crest of the hill. They looked toward the town. It was really unusual to see nothing, no lights anywhere.

And then. "There, did you see it?" Ilya whispered to Petrenko. "It looked like a flashlight. There, there it is again."

He squinted his eyes until they were no more than slits. They both heard the noise, not the sound of the normal ebb and flow of the sea, but something more steady. Their eyes, now adjusted to the darkness, picked up what looked like a small motorized pontoon boat—another and then another.

"Oh my God," Petrenko gasped. "We're being invaded!"

Just then a rifle shot was heard from behind them accompanied by other shots below and then, people shouting to one another.

"I'm not sure what to do. Yuri, what do you think?"

"I don't know if we'll survive, my friend. Look at us. We look just like them. If we take off our suits, these nuts up here will probably shoot us."

They could hear automatic machine gun fire returned toward the island and the flap, flap sound of a helicopter in the distance.

"We can't hide. Our best bet is to try and make it to the boat, take these clothes off, sit with our hands up and pray."

"You mean all of our clothes? Naked?"

"You got it my friend. They sure will see we aren't armed."

"Get out of here, we've been found out!" screamed a worker on the dock. Others shoved each other out of the way to find an open space in the departing boats, throwing boxes overboard to make room. Many jumped into the water and blindly started swimming out to sea toward the freighter.

The Major grabbed Petrov by the arm. "Get the crates, the crates, go, go! I'll meet you at the boat."

"No, Major, you have to help me carry them, they're too heavy."

By the time they reached the boat, three workers were getting into it. The Major yelled at them to get out of his boat. When they refused, he shot them instantly. He needed no companions. There was only room for him and his precious cargo. Nothing was more important than his cargo. The two of them threw the bodies overboard into the sea.

The Major anxiously waited, guarding the boat while Petrov went back and retrieved the remaining boxes and then handed him the last one.

As the Major started the motor and pulled away, Petrov saluted. "Good luck, Major."

Vorack watched the figure of Petrov diminish and disappear as the boat sped out to the open sea. He turned off the running lights. He could see Crook Neck Island in the distance and headed in that direction. He heard the approaching helicopters and hoped he could be out of sight by the time they made it to Fisher Island. As he passed the freighter, he saw the panic up on deck. They were closing the loading doors below, stranding several boats in the water between the ship and the island. He could hear the engines engage.

The freighter hoped to make it into international waters before being intercepted.

The Major looked at his watch: 2:50a.m. It won't

be long now, he thought. He kept looking behind him, over his shoulder. He pulled back on the throttle momentarily and spun around and set the engine to idle. He waited. He was agitated. Petrov should have set off the explosives by now, he thought.

The sudden noise was deafening. A flash of man-made lightning split the sky as a large section of the west side of the island violently exploded and fell into the sea. The noise made Vorack cover his ears. Bright red flames shot high into the night sky, illuminating the town shore line and dropping fiery debris on the deck of the hapless *Levongrad*. He watched as one of the helicopters, caught in the updraft, explode in mid-air. He could see two other helicopters approaching swiftly. The violent rocking of his boat caused his engine to sputter and stop.

"Damn," he shouted.

Before Vorack could restart the motor and move his boat toward the waiting submarine, a bright ray of light illuminated him and the waters around him. He looked up, shielding his eyes from the blinding light and realized one of the helicopters had him pinned down. The more he tried to restart the flooded motor, the more frustrated he became. He couldn't believe how close he was to getting away. If he just hadn't stopped to look back.

At the south end of the island, Ilya and Petrenko were blown out of the boat by the explosion. Petrenko was knocked unconscious, hitting his head on the side of the boat. Ilya managed to keep his friend afloat until a hand reached down to him from a pontoon boat and pulled them both aboard. Ilya blushed as she handed him her jacket.

Jake had just climbed up on the rocks when the explosion occurred. He was reaching down to help Grace out of the boat when a rock slide caught them both by surprise, filling the boat with stones and dirt. Grace never let go of Jake's hand and the two of them landed in the shallow water. They covered their heads as the debris kept falling.

"Keep down, I'm coming your way," someone yelled. Jenkins suddenly rose out of the water. He pulled off his flippers and mask and ran over toward them. "What the hell happened? No one said anything about expecting explosives. Are you hurt?"

"I'm OK. I think Grace has hurt her arm and she's got a nasty gash on her forehead."

Just then, Jake heard Clyde's voice coming from the water somewhere behind them. When he turned around, he could just about make out the structure of the patrol boat thirty feet from shore.

"Jake, Jake, a helicopter pilot's been trying to call you," he shouted. "Vorack's in a speed boat up around the south end. The Major's pinned down for the moment. He's flooded his motor. The helicopter has its spotlight on him. Come with me. Good thing I was in the second wave. Sam's coming to pick you up in the dinghy. He'll bring you back here. We need to hurry."

"Clyde," Jake yelled back. "Have your phone ready. I want you to make contact with that helicopter."

"Grace, tell me how to get ahold of the helicopter pilot."

"Jake, tell Clyde to use this coded number, 555-789-4033," Grace answered. "It'll get you through to someone who can do that."

Jake looked up and saw Sam suddenly appear out of the darkness. Jake ran over to Grace sitting on a pile of rocks. Bending down, he kissed her quickly. "I don't want to leave you alone."

"Go, Go, now! Jenkins will stay with me. I'll be OK."

"I'll see to it someone will come to get you, Grace. Won't be long," he called to her as he climbed into the small boat.

She gave him the thumbs up.

"Hurry up, Sam. We don't have much time. We can't let that SOB get away this time."

Clyde dropped the ladder over the side to the two of them. After Jake climbed up, he gave Clyde the coded number. "Tell the agents in the helicopter not to shoot Vorack. We're on our way. We need backup. Send someone to the southeast side of the island to pick up Special Agent Cooper asap. She needs medical attention. Now c'mon let's go get him."

Clyde pushed the throttle forward as they sped off in pursuit. As they rounded the south end of the island, they saw the Major's boat drifting in circles as he frantically tried to restart the engine. Jake looked back at the part of the island not effected by the blast and saw that most of the other teams had made it onto the shore and were moving forward to secure what was left. Through his binoculars, he could just make out the Russians being rounded up, their hands in the air in surrender. It wouldn't be long before the third wave would arrive and haul them off to a secure area they'd set up in the town recreation center. He glanced back at town and saw lights on everywhere.

"Give it all you've got, Clyde. We're almost there."

With the bright light and the noise from the helicopter above him, Vorack didn't hear Jake and Clyde approaching until they were practically on top of him. The Major reached down in front of him and grabbed his rifle ready to shoot, but the rocking movement of the boat caused him to lose his balance. Vorack fell to one side, hitting his head on the side rail of the hull.

The patrol boat loomed over Vorack, who was back on his feet again, rifle in hand. Jake jumped down onto the deck. The Major got off one shot before Jake grabbed him. The rifle fell from his hands. Vorack lost his footing and landed flat on his back. Jake pulled him upright, turned him around and cuffed him. Sam jumped down to help.

"Get him down again. I need to tie his feet."

Vorack's legs flew in all directions, kicking as hard as he could, almost knocking Sam over before he could be restrained.

"Good work, Sam."

Vorack swore in Russian the whole time. Jake looked up and gave the helicopter crew the thumbs up.

By this time a half dozen other boats began encircling the scene. Jake looked up again and recognized Quinn waving down at him from the hovering helicopter above Vorack's floundering boat.

"Overjoyed to see you got him, Sheriff," she shouted at Jake. "He sure doesn't look happy. I'll throw down the sling. Let's hoist him up here and

I'll take him back to the lockup. Strap him in tightly. We don't want to lose him now."

In spite of the rocking boat, Clyde, Sam and Jake were able to strap the struggling, cursing Major into the chair and watched him being hoisted into the helicopter. The angry Vorack lay on the floor of the helicopter, his body contorted, as he struggled with his restraints.

Quinn leaned out of the door again and gave the three of them the thumbs up. She yelled down to Jake over the din of the surrounding noise. "Great job. I know you have a lot to do out here yet. See you when you come back to shore."

Quinn waved at Jake as the helicopter headed to the mainland.

Back on the patrol boat, Jake went out on deck and looked back at the island. Ash was still falling from the explosion. From what he could tell, surprisingly, most of the island was still intact.

"Clyde, call Grace right away and tell her we got him."

"No problem."

"Hey, Sam. Give me your phone. Mine's in the bottom of the drink. I've got to call the Coast Guard. They're out searching for that sub that was supposed to be here as well. We want to be sure the *Levongrad* doesn't leave its present location."

Jake looked through his binoculars toward Crook Neck Island and saw a helicopter scanning the water. He figured if there'd been a sub, it was long gone by now. The *Levongrad* seemed to have stopped just before it could reach the safety of international waters. He called the Coast Guard. He was right. No sub.

235

"Jake, I just got a call from Grace. She and some agents have boarded the *Levongrad*. She's got back-up from the Coast Guard too. Hold on, Jake. Let me see if I can reach the helicopter pilot monitoring the *Levongrad*."

While Clyde moved back into the cabin to get away from the noise, Jake told Sam to take Vorack's boat back to the dock and get help to see it was secure until they could search it in the morning. Most of the other boats moved out as well. Jake called down to Turner and Flynn not to leave—wait for him to join them. Clyde returned and told him the pilot had seen a woman confronting a group of men. Yeah, a lot of hands raised on deck now. Looked as if she and her men have everything tied up.

"She's something else, Jake. Isn't she one amazing woman."

"You bet, Clyde—she is amazing."

By now, lights were on all over town. The explosion had triggered the town's warning sirens. People in bathrobes, with flashlights and binoculars flooded into the streets. They were kept behind barricades now lining the sidewalks on Main Street. The National Guard reassured the people they were safe. All eyes were focused on the dull red glow illuminating the central section of Fisher Island. Everyone was asking questions that had no answers for them. Rumors were rampant.

A bewildered Old Man Tinker sat wrapped in a blanket on the front steps of his now mud and sand covered front porch. He was in shock. The ocean surge caused by the sinking of part of the far side of the island had scuttled three of his rental boats. He wondered about his future as well as Caswell Bay's. He couldn't imagine there would ever be another Summerfair. Certainly, anyone who had travelled here for a restful vacation, would never return. What will happen to his quiet little town now? What in the world caused Fisher Island to explode and who were all those people out there?

Fifty-four

"Clyde, I think I'll go with Turner and Flynn and check out the rest of the island," Jake said. "Their boat's more maneuverable. You go on back to the station. See you there in about an hour."

Soon the three of them swung the boat around and headed toward the collapsed west side of the island. The explosion left a lot of debris in the water and it was difficult to get anywhere close to shore. Jake could see the island had to cool down more before they could investigate it further. They picked up an injured Russian struggling to stay afloat in the choppy water, throwing a blanket around him.

"Did you come off the boat or off the island?"

"The island," he said weakly.

"What's your name?"

"Petrov."

Up ahead the other Russians were being put into several launches that arrived in the third wave.

"Let's get Petrov here over there to join his comrades."

The sky started to lighten Sunday morning as they handed Petrov over to the Coast Guard. Jake scanned the length of the island taking in the scope of the damage. The island held up better than he expected. He hoped they could find some remnant of the base when they came back later. The important thing was, they'd captured Vorack and some of his henchmen. He turned the boat around and the three of them sped back to the mainland.

As they entered the marina, he saw an empty patrol boat and the Major's boat being guarded by an agent he hadn't met yet. He hurried to tie up his boat and get to over to the department.

"Quite a night, guys," he said to Sam and Turner climbing into the driver's seat of the parked cruiser. "What a day ahead."

Jake circled around the main part of town. He was able to glance down Main Street and saw it filled with people and the barricades in place. Good work, he thought. Yellow tape cordoned off the tented areas. Some of the artists who were staying in town were packing up and officers patrolled the perimeter to prevent looting. That was a wise decision, he thought. For the most part, everything looked under control.

He noticed the lights on in the Hungry Goose. He imagined they were giving out coffee and doughnuts to the security teams. He could use a cup of coffee himself. He was anxious to get back to the station not only to interview Vorack, but to hear any news they might have from Grace. When they arrived at the sheriff's department and went inside, he was surprised to see her standing in the doorway of his office talking with Clyde.

"How'd you get here before me?" he said hurrying across the room.

He hugged her so tightly, she could hardly breathe. He didn't care who saw them. He was so grateful they'd both come through in one piece.

Quinn came up behind him. "Ahem, when you come up for air, I'd like to talk to you too." She laughed. It felt good to laugh.

"OK, OK, let's come into my office and go over what happens next. Ann, did Vorack give you any trouble?"

"You've got to be kidding. He's still mad as hell. He says he won't tell us anything."

"Well, Grace, what do you think? I'll bet he's going to be surprised to see you!"

Grace smiled broadly. "I can't wait."

"Hey, Jake, what a night!" Clyde said, "I just received a call from Director Johnson telling me that two of the men they pulled out of the water after the explosion turned out to be a Russian scientist, Dr. Yuri Petrenko and a Russian defector named Ilya Kostalow. They're taking them to Portland for debriefing. He'll be in touch."

"Thanks, Clyde. Listen, ask Tina to find out where they're holding a Russian named Petrov. Grace said he was Vorack's right-hand man and could give us a lot of info. I'd like him brought here asap. Be sure he's cuffed. We don't want to lose him on the way over. Thanks. Let me know when he arrives."

"Well, Sheriff, ready to interview our guest of honor?" Ann asked enthusiastically. "I'll be watching in the observation room. I can't miss seeing the look on his face when Grace walks in."

When Jake opened the interrogation room door, he saw the seated Vorack shackled to the table, his head fallen down on his chest. He looked as if he was asleep. Amazing, Jake thought.

"Hello, Major. Welcome to your new home."

Vorack's head jerked up at the sound of Jake's voice.

Vorack glared back at Jake and was about to say something sarcastic in return, when Jake continued. "I have someone here who wants to speak with you." He stepped aside letting a smiling Grace stand in the doorway in full view of the Major.

"Surprise!"

Vorack's eyes widened and for a moment his mouth slackened in shock.

"You. You're supposed to be dead. You killed Boris, didn't you, you—"

"Now, now Major. It was your pal Dimitri who killed Boris. I didn't have the pleasure," Grace said as she walked into the room closing the door behind her.

"Karl and Gregor were supposed to dispose of you. Gregor told me they had."

"Oh, Major, Gregor is such a liar. He'll do anything for immunity. As for Karl, he met his maker thanks to the good sheriff here. But more importantly, Gregor helped us find you."

"He'll get his in time. I'll see to that,"the Major sneered.

"Probably so. But better yet, we have you right here. We also have your precious spybirds and your toxin. Not a happy ending to your plans, right?"

241

"I have nothing more to say to you or your sheriff friend, Grace Cooper."

"That's Special Agent Grace Cooper of the FBI."

Again Vorack's face went pale. How could he have been so completely taken in by this woman? She'd come with impeccable credentials. As soon as he could, he'd find out who was responsible.

His thoughts were diverted by a knock on the door. Jake went over and opened it and saw Tina standing there. She said something to Jake that Vorack couldn't make out. He saw Jake look up and motion to someone.

"Well, Major, this is your special day. We have someone else joining your little party."

"Come in—come in. It's alright. Don't be nervous."

Petrov now stood in the doorway.

"What—what?" stammered Vorack. "Petrov. I thought you were dead. How did you manage to escape the blast?"

"I didn't set off all the explosives, only two, and I ran away," he said. "I was afraid. I thought of my wife and little boy in Russia and—"

"You coward!" screamed the enraged Major, struggling to stand up. "I thought I could count on you, you of all people."

"Petrov has been very helpful," Jake said. "There's a good chance he'll be seeing his family soon. We have enough on you, Major, to send you away for a long time in one of our federal prisons. Oh, I forgot to mention. We've also detained your special friend, Dr. Petrenko, who's being interrogated by the FBI as we speak. And, you may be lucky enough to run into another good friend of yours soon too, Bob Knox, once the two of you are behind bars."

Major Vorack looked down at his shackled hands. Whatever hope he'd had of escaping the trap he'd fallen into, whatever defiant energy he had left in him before the interview, had disappeared.

"Nothing further to say, Major?" Grace asked.

No response.

"Get him out of here," Jake motioned to Ben, who'd been watching with a grinning Ann behind the two-way glass above the table.

After the interrogation, the FBI transported Vorack to a maximum security facility in upstate New York to await trial. With the evidence they collected from the boat and the information given out by Petrov and Petrenko, they felt they had an airtight case against the Major.

Jake sat with his feet up on his desk and looked over at Grace, who had fallen asleep curled up in the chair across from him. He wondered when she'd slept last. He glanced down at his watch, which had stopped working when they hit the water. What time was it?

The squad room was empty except for Clyde and Tina. Ben and the others were told to go home, get some rest and come back later at 1p.m. Fortunately, none of his department's men suffered any injury in the invasion. It was going to take a long time to restore the Bay to the quiet little seaside village it once was.

Grace slowly opened her eyes. "Can we go home now?"

Jake walked over to her and took her hand and lifted her up into his arms.

"Yes, my brave young woman. I can't stay awake much longer myself."

On their way out of the office, Jake went over to where Clyde sat with his feet propped up on his desk sound asleep. He didn't have the heart to wake him. He went into Tina's office and told her that he and Grace were going back to the beach house for a while. He'd be back at the department by 10 a.m. Happily, the FBI Director had postponed their meeting until noon.

Tina told him to take as much time as he needed. She'd take care of things. She'd only awaken Clyde if necessary.

Fifty-five

Four hours later, Jake stirred in his sleep, hearing the sound of Rex barking next door. His body was still wrapped in the warmth of Grace next to him under the down comforter. Half awake, he turned over and kissed her gently on the forehead. When she opened her eyes, she couldn't believe the wave of happiness that swept over her.

She reached out and put her hand on his face. She felt so blessed.

"Jake, tell me you love me—and—you know, what you started to say to me just before I went out to the island. I stopped you. Remember?"

"Yes, I do," he said.

"I want you to know I love you, Grace Cooper. I want to be with you. I want to wake up every morning and see you next to me. Stay with me forever."

"Yes, yes, yes, Sheriff Jake Mason, I accept."

About the Author

I grew up in Connecticut and went to Pratt Institute in New York. My goal was to become an art director. It was there I met my future husband, moved to Ohio and had two sons.

After my boys were in school, I became a secretary in an ad agency, went on to complete my education and became an elementary school teacher. The art teacher there inspired me to go into lapidary work. I took several courses, ending up at the Cleveland Institute of Art. There, I learned how to enamel and create finished pieces of jewelry. I began selling my designs in galleries and at art shows. One day, I sketched a trapeze artist suspended from tiny black beads. From that first piece, I designed a line of jewelry based on the circus, a joyous memory of my childhood growing up in Bridgeport, Ct., home of PT Barnum.

Early in my life, my father introduced me to his

favorite fictional sleuth, Sherlock Holmes, opening the door to mystery and adventure. Each summer, we'd head to Maine to revisit my Dad's boyhood home at Flying Point. Maine seemed a natural setting for my imaginary adventure.

Over the years, I've written poetry and newspaper travel articles describing trips my artist husband and I had taken to exotic places around the world. A recent trip back to Maine inspired me to sit down one day and begin writing this, my first novel. I've enjoyed bringing Jake and Grace to life. As they used to say on the old radio mystery shows, stay tuned for their next exciting adventure.